OH-OH!

Suddenly, a familiar figure appeared. I would know that rosy-cheeked, blank face anywhere. It was Margaret Wentworth, from my hometown. My reflective mood vanished to be replaced by panic. I quickly buried my nose in my notebook. I could just imagine her careening into the union and shrieking, "Deborah Susan, what have you done to your hair?" I wiped my sweaty palms on my jeans and stared at my notes.

"Studying already?"

I looked up to see James Stuart looming over me. He was holding a cup of coffee and a danish. He slid into the booth and propped one foot up next to me. I was painfully aware of his closeness.

"Don't worry so much."

I was stung. Deborah Susan might worry, but Dusty never did. Never.

I tossed my notebook aside carelessly. "I wasn't worried," I said. "I make it a point not to worry."

DUSTY BRANNIGAN

JANICE HARRELL

AN AVON FLARE BOOK

DUSTY BRANNIGAN is an original publication of Avon Books. This work has never before appeared in book form.

AVON BOOKS
A division of
The Hearst Corporation
1350 Avenue of the Americas
New York, New York 10019

Copyright © 1993 by Janice Harrell
Published by arrangement with the author
Library of Congress Catalog Card Number: 92-97299
ISBN: 0-380-76113-0
RL: TK

First Avon Flare Printing: May 1993

AVON FLARE TRADEMARK REG. U.S. PAT. OFF. AND IN OTHER COUNTRIES, MARCA REGISTRADA, HECHO EN U.S.A.

Printed in the U.S.A.

RA 10 9 8 7 6 5 4 3 2 1

Chapter One

I have never been able to stand books where the heroine is a nitwit. You know, where the real estate agent tells her the house is haunted and she says, "I'll take it for three months. Sign me up for the winter, when the fog rolls in." It's even worse when the heroine falls for some cute guy in tight jeans and doesn't catch on that he's sleaze until page 200 even though sleaze has been oozing from his pores and glowing like kryptonite since page ten. The whole time you want to scream at her "Don't be such an idiot!"

I promise you this is not going to be that kind of book. I am not an idiot. When I was a baby, perfect strangers used to comment not just on my blue eyes but on how intelligent I looked. Somewhat more recently, I blew the top off the SATs. I don't mean to brag, but this fact happens to be relevant to the story. If it hadn't been for those SAT scores, my whole life would have been different.

It all began the first week in May of my senior year, when our guidance counselor, Mr. Pringle, called me into his office. He was polishing his glasses and the light was shining on his bald spot. On the wall behind him was a poster of a rainbow with the message, "Life is not a problem to be solved, but a mystery to enjoy."

"Deborah," he said, "a representative of Blake College has been in touch with me." He pursed his lips thoughtfully. "She asked to see all the students with high SAT scores who had not made a definite decision about college."

As Mr. Pringle well knew, the only reason I had not made a definite decision was because there aren't all that many possibilities when you don't have a cent and your parents aren't capable of filling out a financial aid form. As a matter of fact, when Mr. Pringle called me out of class, I had been sitting in Mrs. Owens's solid geometry class, staring into space while I tried to decide between attending our local technical school and becoming the first virgin ever to end it all on Lover's Leap.

"Blake College is only four years old," Mr. Pringle went on, "but it's beginning to establish a good reputation. It's a small liberal arts school with ties to the Presbyterian Church. Because Blake is so new, they are offering special inducements to attract high-scoring students. I explained to them about your difficulties with the financial aid form, and they seemed to feel something could be worked out. At any rate, you might want to talk with their representative, Ms. Martin."

Talk with her? I was ready to kiss her feet.

I later found out there were only three "undecided" kids with SAT scores high enough to interest the Blake representative—Larry Highsmith, Charlene Miller, and me. Larry was set on becoming a race car driver and Charlene was going to marry her boyfriend Jerry as soon as she got up the nerve to tell her parents. So that left me to talk with the Blake representative alone. Luckily, authority figures do not intimidate me. I attribute this to my parents having been the first authority figures I encountered. At an early age I learned that the people in charge often don't have a clue.

I met with Ms. Martin that same afternoon in Mr. Pringle's office. She looked like a fullback in drag and smoked enough to kipper herrings. Her teeth were yellow and she wore lace-up shoes, but tough as this lady looked, she cooed over my SAT scores. She assured me my parents didn't have to fuss over the financial aid form but should just put down any old thing. I warmed to her instantly.

I took the forms home to my parents. "They'll accept an estimate," I pleaded. "Just make something up. Anything." Finally, they agreed to take a stab at it. I knew it was going to be hard for them. My parents were the sort of people who never balanced their checkbook. Instead they called up the bank every now and then to find out how much was left in the account and then were surprised when a thick stack of checks bounced every month. They had no idea about the total of the family's "undischarged debts" or about the "extraordinary expenses" the financial aid form was so curious about. Very likely they preferred not to know. We lived on my father's small salary as a clerk at Higgins Hardware and the financial picture in our household was all too bleak if examined closely.

"I don't know," Mom said as she bent over the table that evening, staring at the form. She chewed meditatively on her pencil. "They certainly want a lot of stuff here. Frank, do you know what your yearly salary is?"

"Take-home pay?"

"No, they seem to want the whole thing. I don't know why. We never see what they take out. It's not as if it actually is income."

Toby tugged at Mom's shirttails. I saw that he had been decorating his face with a Magic Marker again. "Would somebody fix me a hot dog?" he whimpered.

"In a minute, dear."

"There must be an old pay stub around here somewhere," said Dad. He got up and rustled through the stack of clippings, store coupons, and bills littering the bureau that stood in our living-dining area. An entry blank for a contest promising a free trip to Tahiti fluttered to the floor. My mother was always filling out those things.

"They said you could just estimate it," I reminded Mom.

"Right. Now, let's see—how many weeks are in a year?" she asked.

"Won't somebody fix me a hot dog?" Toby repeated.

"Can't we turn the television off while we work on this?" I asked.

"I think Peggy was watching something," Mom said.

Somebody was always watching something at our house. If you clicked off the TV you'd hear, "Hey, I was watching that," even though no one was in sight and the protest came from the other end of the house. I could only conclude that in our family, "watching television" was some sort of spiritual state not evident to the eye of the unbeliever.

Our 28-inch color TV set was the only luxury in our house, which may have been why my family was determined to get the most out of it. It never got turned off. It droned monotonously, unendingly, as if the family had subconsciously decided it was the pulsing heart of our house. It got so hot from constant use that once when Peggy left her crayons on top of it, they were melted into a puddle by the time she remembered where she had left them. Not the least of my dreams about college was that it would get me away from the television set.

"What do you imagine they mean by 'equity'?" Mom asked.

"Let me look at that," said Dad.

Some hours later, the financial aid form was smudged with catsup (Mom had finally fixed Toby's hot dog). It was also dog-eared and entirely covered with parentheses and asterisks designed to indicate that the figures my parents had filled in were estimates, wild guesses. Basically, it was fiction. Still, I did have a financial aid application—of a sort. And I had to admit they had done their best. Evidently they were not, as I had suspected in my darkest moments, plotting to keep me at home so they could make use of my earnings at Burger King.

I mailed the form at once and a few weeks later a letter came from Blake College saying I had been accepted with a grant for full tuition, room, and board plus twenty dollars a month spending money. I considered this absolute proof that I had a fairy godmother.

Needless to say, I was rigid with excitement. It

wasn't just that I was excited about getting a good education, you understand—I wanted to get away from home. I wanted it with the kind of white hot burning desire that other people reserve for members of the opposite sex. To understand why, you first have to picture our house.

It was built in the forties when there was a shortage of building materials. This might explain why everything about it was, like my family, vaguely inadequate. The metal roof had no overhang, so rain came in open windows. The space heater in the hall was so unreliable we could have stayed warm just as well by running in place, and with the pine floor raised off the ground on cement blocks, wind whistled underneath and kept the floor icy in winter. In short, the house offered only marginal shelter from the elements.

There wasn't much peace at our house either. Besides the noise of the television set and the yelling you have any time seven people live crammed into a small space, there was the problem of stray cats. They liked to set up housekeeping under the house and we were always being awakened by the sounds of their love life, which was, I might add, a darn sight more interesting than my own. During the winter the house rang with the bronchial coughs of my four younger brothers and sisters, and with their allergic sneezes during the rest of the year. The Brannigans were not a very sturdy lot. Medical bills and the resulting rush to lending companies for the needed cash was part of what had helped sink us financially.

Recently I had noticed that the whole house was sagging slightly in the middle. It was as if it were bowed down by the weight of my family's troubles. I looked up in it as an omen. I had to get out of that house before I sank with the rest of them. I didn't even feel very guilty about wanting to leave. With the seven of us sharing three bedrooms and one bath, heck, I was doing the rest of them a favor.

Before, college had seemed as shimmeringly romantic and unattainable as Xanadu. But now, thanks to my SAT scores and an incredible stroke of luck, I was going. I was stepping out of squalor and into a new life.

The first thing I intended to do when I went away was to change my name. Deborah Susan Brannigan was to vanish without a trace. The name Deborah Susan, to my mind, strongly suggested poverty, chastity, and obedience. In other words, it reeked of the life I intended to escape.

It proved harder than I thought to come up with a new name. So many of the good ones had already been used by the most popular girls in my class— Paige, Dawn, Tiffany. I wanted something that could belong to me alone, something a little unusual, but definitely not anything weird or literary. Esmerelda, for example, was out. So was Portia.

It took a while, but I finally hit on one that was perfect—Dusty. It had a good feel to it. To me the name Dusty suggested a girl wearing cut-offs and sitting on a fence under a spreading oak tree. If she had a car, it was a secondhand Ford. If she had a dog, it was a mutt. I pictured her boyfriend as having biceps, a grin, and grease under his fingernails.

It goes without saying that Dusty did not have a messed-up family and she did not live very tensely on a marginal income. In fact, nothing about Dusty was marginal. She had grown up in the bosom of Middle America. I was crazy about her already.

After I made the decision about my name, everything else fell into place. During the rest of the long hot summer while I was dishing out hamburgers, the band of my Burger King cap damp with sweat, I kept picturing the girl I was to become, rehearsing Dusty in my mind so I would have her perfected by the time I went away to school.

At the end of August, Mom and Dad drove me to St. Petersburg to the Blake campus. I had tried to think of a way to get out of having them take me, but there wasn't any, so I just kept telling myself that they didn't look that different from all the other parents. Nobody could know we did our shopping at the Salvation Army Thrift Shop.

"My baby," sniffled Mom when we arrived. "My baby is going away to college!" Her flyaway hair was ruffled by a faint breeze from the bay.

The Blake campus was not ivy-covered, but I hadn't expected that, since the college was only a few years old. Broad expanses of fine-bladed grass surrounded new brick buildings. A few thorny trees dotted the lawn at wide intervals. Beyond the college buildings the waters of the bay sparkled, and some black-headed gulls wheeled around the rooftops of the dorms, squawking.

"You don't have to come up to the room with me," I said.

"You need help with your suitcases," said Dad. "And we want to meet your roommate. We want to be sure you're all settled in before we go."

"I can manage the suitcases," I said quickly. "I

8

can make two trips. Three trips. However many trips it takes."

But Dad had already grabbed two suitcases and was heading up the walk to Grant dormitory. The girl's dorms, buildings no bigger than houses, had been built in clusters around fenced patios.

I followed Dad into the dorm, relieved to see that among the girls who were struggling with suitcases and trunks in the hallway there were a number in jeans. A few even had bandannas around their hair as I did.

My room was on the second floor overlooking the road that separated the dorms from the cafeteria. The two beds in the room had already been made up since the college provided linen service. The room's only other furnishings were two starkly modern bureaus and matching desks. I walked across the room and looked out the plate-glass window. On the lawn below, I could see girls and their parents carrying lamps, clothes hangers, and stuffed animals. The road that ran between the dorms and the cafeteria was lined with parked cars. Behind me, I heard Mom blowing her nose loudly. "It's kind of like a motel in here, isn't it?" she said.

"No sign of your roommate yet," said Dad. "I guess that means you get your choice of beds."

I cleared my throat. "Right. Well, don't feel like you have to hang around. I know you've got a long drive home."

"Don't you want us to help you unpack and get settled in?" asked Dad.

"No, I don't think so," I said. I was doing my best to be subtle about getting rid of them. I didn't want to hurt their feelings. I smiled. "I won't have anything else to do all day. I can take care of the unpacking."

"Well, if you're sure," said Mom. "I guess we had better be getting back to the boys. I don't like to leave Peggy alone with them any longer than we have to."

In point of fact, it was another fifteen minutes before they actually left. You would have thought they were trying to get in *The Guinness Book of World Records* for the longest good-bye. I just wished they would *go*.

Finally Mom hugged me. "Now be sure and write."

Dad slipped a five-dollar bill into my palm. "Take care of yourself, baby."

I smiled weakly.

When at last they were gone, I leaned on the closed door and breathed a silent prayer of thanks that my roommate had not shown up yet. The new me—Dusty—was not going to have parents. At least, if she had parents, she never talked about them. And one thing was certain—hers were not at all like mine. they did not wear shoes that looked as if they had been picked up at a garage sale, and they did not call her "baby." Dusty's parents were shadowy figures who were very much in the background. Perhaps they lived in Iowa.

Moving fast, I dumped my clothes on the bed and promptly hid my cheap luggage in a small room I found off the hall which was marked "luggage storage." I did not want to be known as the girl with the cardboard luggage.

When I got back to the room, I stowed my clothes in the drawers and arranged my makeup on the surface of the bureau. In the mirror hanging over the bureau, my anxious face stared back at me. Remembering how secure Dusty was supposed to be, I forced myself to smile. My smile was not very confident yet, but this was, after all, only Dusty's first day.

The room seemed frighteningly empty and my heartbeat quickened. I realized I was panicked by the silence. In our house, even if you were in the bathroom, chances were somebody was hammering on the door complaining that you were taking too long. And except for the bathroom, I had probably never been in a room by myself in my whole life. I was spooked.

I heard a girl's voice call, "Up here, Mom." I reminded myself that people were moving in all over the dorm, and I would get to know some of them soon. I wasn't really alone, and there was nothing to panic about. I whipped off my bandanna and stared at myself in the mirror and swallowed. The new me was going to take some getting used to, but I was glad I had managed to barricade myself in the family bathroom long enough late the night before to put on the finishing touch. Deborah Susan Brannigan had wimpy, light brown hair, but Dusty was a platinum blonde. Out of deference to my parents' feelings, I had thought it best to conceal this important change with a bandanna until they left.

The hair was all wrong, I realized suddenly. It had a sort of Marilyn Monroe effect and retro was definitely not the look I was after. I reached for my nail scissors and began cutting. No sooner had I swept the hair clippings off the bureau and into the trash can when I realized someone was at the door.

"This is it, Enid," someone said. The door opened and a small woman came in. "You must be Enid's roommate," she said, smiling at me. "I'm Enid's mother." She looked like Betty Crocker but rounder and softer looking.

My mouth was dry so I just nodded.

A lean boy with straight, dark blond hair backed into the room with Enid's footlocker. He shook the hair out of his eyes. "Take it easy, Dennis," he said. "It's a tight squeeze in here."

"Enid, honey," her mother warbled, "I don't think that footlocker is going to fit in here."

The other end of the footlocker appeared, supported by Dennis, who was bony and uncommonly tall. He looked intelligent, but that may just have been his glasses.

After them came my new roommate. Her glasses were perched on a jutting, rather aquiline nose, but everything else about her, from her porcelain skin to her light blue eyes was delicate and neat. She was so fine boned as to be bird-like, and her fair hair curled evenly under at the ends, like the hair of the king on the deck of cards. Incongruously, she was dressed in cut-offs and an outsized sweat shirt. I later learned her tastes ran to big sweaters, padded jackets and shoulder pads whenever possible. She probably hoped they would make her look bigger.

I stared at her, impressed in spite of myself at anyone who was willing to go off to college with a name like Enid.

She pulled the trunk open and began throwing the clothes out on her bed. "Let me just dump this and we'll get this thing out of here. This room is little, isn't it? But never mind, we'll manage. Hold up, guys, I wonder if you could just help us get the trunk back to the car?"

Clothes seemed to be flying in all directions, but in a matter of minutes the trunk was empty and the boys were backing out of the room with it. Enid beamed. "Thanks, guys. I really do appreciate it."

"Any time," said the tall boy, smiling at her over his shoulder. "Maybe I'll see you around."

As soon as the door closed behind the boys, she threw herself down on the bed. "I know I should have introduced everybody, but I couldn't remember the other boy's name."

"His name was James, dear," said her mother. "I remember."

"Oh, right. I'm terrible about names. The tall one was a senior, Dennis Whitley. Didn't you think he was sweet?"

My new roommate was no beauty and I was surprised to see that she seemed to be already making a conquest, but I later realized that Enid was the sort who would always have men in her life.

"You must be Deborah Susan," she said.

"Call me Dusty," I said.

Chapter Two

Even though we had only just met, I had begun to suspect that Enid was the perfect roommate. You only had to look at the way she folded her clothes to see that in her personal habits she was as fastidious as a monk. I was also favorably impressed when she put her cigarette away without a murmur when I explained that smoke bothered my contact lenses.

"You're from Ocala, aren't you?" said Enid. "I met a girl downstairs who was from Ocala. I wish I could remember her name."

I felt chilled. The last thing I needed was to run in to someone who would remind me of the old me.

"She was a tall girl, very blond," Enid went on. "Does that ring a bell?"

"Ocala has a lot of blonds," I said. "It could be anybody." I didn't want Enid to get the idea I was going to rush around trying to find this girl from my hometown because I wasn't. The first time I saw a familiar face I planned to hide.

Suddenly someone stuck her head in our door. "Do you want to come down to my room and have some popcorn? I'm Carol Prentiss, your freshman advisor. I'm trying to round up all my advisees as they come in so we can get acquainted."

Enid and I looked at each other. "Sure," I said.

We followed Carol down the hall to her room feeling humbled. This girl was goddess material. Her voice was low and throaty, her hair honey-colored, and her figure luscious. The only thing about her that was not absolutely perfect was that her thin, high-arched eyebrows didn't seem to belong to her face. I later learned that she was a demon housekeeper. Just as she didn't know when to stop dusting, she didn't know when to stop plucking her eyebrows.

"Is pretty much everybody here already?" asked Enid.

"Well, all my advisees are here, anyway. You two are the last."

Carol's room—which was a single—had a view of the bay. This was the girl who had it all. Everything except decent eyebrows. I glanced quickly at the other four freshmen in the room as Carol introduced us, relieved to see that none of them looked familiar. The news that someone from my hometown was at large on campus had put me on edge.

Two girls, Mandy and Cindy, were sitting demurely at the foot of Carol's bed dressed in full preppie regalia. I pretty much dismissed them at sight. I knew I didn't have the clothes to run with the preppie crowd.

Ann was a smartly dressed redhead with freckles and a broad smile. The fourth girl was called Meg. She was long-legged and wore skintight jeans that zipped at the ankle. Her long soft hair fell over one eye like a curtain, half obscuring her face. "Don't

15

you think it's a shame we don't have coed dorms?" she asked in a whispery voice.

"You can have boys in your room from six to until ten on weeknights and until midnight on the weekends," said Carol. "Most people think that's enough. But once the visiting hours are over the gates are locked. You have to wake up Mrs. Carmichael to get in if you come in late."

"Or you could climb over the fence," said Meg.

"I suppose you could if you had a rappelling hook. What you cannot do," Carol told us, "is prop the fire door open. That's not only against the rules but it's a serious breach in dorm security. We can't leave that door so that any roving mass murderer can walk into the dorm in the middle of the night."

"You mean there are going to be boys all over the dorm from six to ten?" said Ann. "I guess this means I'll have to wash my hair in the morning."

Enid perched on a tapestry footstool and looked about her respectfully. "I love the way you've fixed your room up," she said.

I looked down at the jewel-like tones of the oriental rug at my feet and said nothing. I hoped Enid wasn't going to get big decorating ideas, because a place like this, all in French provincial, was out of my league.

"Thank you," said Carol. "I brought a lot of stuff from home. Some people don't mind the dorm furniture, but I guess I have a strong nesting instinct." She laughed throatily and tucked her bare feet under her. With her jeans she was wearing a peach colored Irish knit sweater that undoubtedly cost more than the total of my spending money for the entire year.

"So, Carol, are you going to tell us which ones are the blow away courses?" Mandy piped up.

"I hate to break it to you, girls, but Blake doesn't have any blow away courses. Besides, the first year you'll be all booked up with core requirements anyway."

"I know," groaned Cindy. "They mailed us our schedule. Practically the only thing I get to choose is which language to take."

Carol reached over to lift off the top of the popper. A kernel popped belatedly and landed on the rug.

"Let's not put butter on it, okay, guys?" said Ann. "Everybody at home that I know gained fifteen pounds her freshman year and I'm determined it won't happen to me, even if it means I have to live on Rye Crisp and apples in my room."

"No sacrifice," commented Carol. She tidily picked up the stray kernel and dropped it in her wastebasket.

"Is the food really that bad?"

"Just imagine eating the same thing day after day, that's all. If it's Wednesday, it must be fried fish. Luckily, there's a place called Lou's across the highway for people who can't face another fried fish."

"I guess you must be a senior," said Enid, "if you're that tired of the food."

"I am absolutely not a senior," said Carol firmly. "I'm a junior. All the seniors were Founding Freshmen, and all the Founding Freshmen are *weird*, definitely weird."

"What about Dennis Whitley?" asked Enid. "Is he weird?"

"Well, no. Dennis is a transfer student, like me,

17

so even though he's a senior, he wasn't really a Founding Freshman. He was at Vanderbilt before, but there was a horrible tragedy in his family and he came home so he could be closer to his parents. I think he goes home to Sarasota every weekend now and helps his father out in the family restaurant."

"What happened?" asked one of the preppies.

"An awful car accident. Maybe you read about it. His brother ran a stop sign and plowed his car right into the side of a bus. Dennis's sister was killed instantly and a gas tank exploded and killed five people on the bus. Dennis's brother is serving time in prison now for manslaughter. It turned out he was dead drunk at the time of the accident."

"How awful!" Mandy said, breathlessly.

"Just a little hint," Carol said. "You don't want to go asking Dennis to go out drinking with you. He's a nut on the subject."

Cindy put in, "But drinking's not allowed on campus anyway, is it?"

"Absolutely not," said Carol crisply, suddenly metamorphosing from cozy friend into Freshman Advisor. "And, of course, under the Honor Code you have to report any violations."

So far I hadn't contributed anything to this discussion. That was because I was trying to figure out what sort of thing a girl like Dusty would say. Whatever you say about changing your image, it must be admitted that, at least at first, it inhibits spontaneity. After careful thought, I decided that Dusty, like Deborah Susan, had a normal supply of human curiosity.

"Tell us about these Founding Freshmen," I said. "What's so weird about them?"

"Everything. Think about it. What kind of kid is going to go to a college the very first year it opens?"

"Brave kids?"

"Weird kids. At first they didn't even have any buildings up out here. The whole college was just on paper. So it didn't exactly get the pick of the college-bound seniors. What they got was a bunch of kids who in one way or another were totally screwed up. Maybe they had terrible family problems or erratic grades. They came here because it was the only place that would take them."

Like me, I thought glumly. I'm one of those Carol would call weird.

She flipped some popcorn in her mouth. Her fingernails were perfect pink ovals and a small diamond winked on her left ring finger. "You can practically tell the Founding Freshmen by looking at them," she said. "There's this slightly gooney look that's definitive. Of course, some of them are awfully smart, but they are definitely weird."

"Then why did you come here?" I asked. "After all, you're only one year behind the Founding Freshmen."

She flashed her ring finger. "To be with my fiancé." She grinned. "He's one of the Founding Freshmen."

Suddenly, I liked her better.

As we were walking back to our room afterward, feeling uncomfortably full of popcorn, Enid said, "Don't you love the way she's done up her room?"

"It's too much."

"You think so? I thought it was lovely," she said, a trace of wistfulness in her voice.

19

"I suppose it's all right. But I think there's something decadent about fancy interior decoration when most of the people in the world don't even have enough to eat. I guess I'd have to call myself antimaterialistic. I don't like to get so wrapped up in things."

Enid pushed open the door to our room. "It's just as well. I could never afford a room like that."

I reflected that only people who are reasonably well off can be comfortable admitting that they're short of money. I, for example, never said that I couldn't afford something. I always said that it "wasn't what I had in mind," or when pressed, that I "didn't want to spend that much money," the implication being that I had masses of cash in numbered Swiss accounts and wasn't buying purely as a matter of principle.

"Isn't that awful about Dennis's sister?" Enid said, kicking her shoes off. "I know how he must feel. My father was killed in a car accident five years ago on Christmas Eve. It's something you never get over. Never." Her eyes were shiny.

"It's not too great about his brother being in prison, either."

"His poor parents. It's just awful." She dabbed at her face with a tissue. "Goodness, I feel so grungy after moving all that junk in, I think I'm going to change for dinner."

Sniffling a little, she got a shirt and skirt out of her closet and laid them on the bed. Then she pulled panty hose out of her drawer and began wiggling into them. "So tell me about yourself, Dusty."

"Well, I come from a large family," I began. "I have three brothers and a sister."

"You're so lucky," said Enid. "I've always wanted to have a lot of brothers. I just have one younger sister and we have really different interests. Of course I love her, but we don't have a lot in common."

"My brothers can be fun sometimes," I said.

"I guess having all those brothers give you a lot of insight into how boys think."

"Maybe so," I said. I thought of Toby, his face covered with Magic Marker, Tom, his diapers drooping, and Frank Jr. with his ambition to have the most Masters of the Universe creatures on our block. In the past I had not found they contributed to my understanding of the male sex, but maybe having brothers had some subliminal effect that was only now going to benefit me. I hoped that was it. Taking a deep breath I launched into fiction. "Maybe so. I've always had girlfriends, but some of my best friends are boys. I'm basically a laid-back kind of person. I spend a lot of time sitting on fences and kicking cans around." What I wanted to emphasize was that I was not at all like Deborah Susan, who spent most of her time worrying. "And as you know I come from a small town, so I guess I'm just a typical Middle American type. What about you?"

"Well, Lakeland isn't exactly a metropolis either. Several kids I know from high school are here, but I'm going to try not to spend much time with them. After all, college is supposed to broaden your horizons, right? I don't want to go on just the way I did in high school."

"Oh, absolutely. I couldn't agree more."

She slipped the blouse over her head. "You aren't going to change for dinner?"

I considered my limited wardrobe. "I don't think so," I said. "I try to keep my life as simple as possible. I don't want to get all caught up in superficialities."

"Oh, right, I remember. You're nonmaterialistic. Well, you're ready then?" Enid ran a brush through her fair hair. "I wonder if we should go see if Mandy and Cindy and Meg and Ann want to go with us?" She shrugged. "Oh, I guess we'll see them over there."

I was pleased to have taken my first, halting steps as Dusty. Maybe the self-portrait I had sketched for Enid was pure fiction, but it had contained no statements that could flatly be disproved. I didn't think it would be too hard to maintain the image of a wholesome, laid-back, all-American girl with no personal problems. But while I was trying to present a picture of perfect cool, inside me a shrill little voice was shrieking, "You're at college! Can you believe it?" I was almost overcome by the glamour of actually being a college woman. Me! At college! It was as if I were stepping into a video of somebody else's life.

When Enid and I were going through the line at the cafeteria we saw Carol waving at us. So as soon as we had gotten our food, we took our trays over to the long table where she was sitting with her fiancé. As far as I could tell he didn't look a bit weird, even if he had been a Founding Freshman. Just outside the big cafeteria window, I could see a cement block pump house and beyond a collection of sailboats was moored near a bridge where a creek fed into the bay. I wondered if I would have a chance to go out on a sailboat. That would have been even more like living in a video. But something told me they would check to make sure you could swim before they let you, so probably the answer was no.

Dennis and his friend James suddenly appeared at our table. "Are you all settled in?" Dennis asked us, pulling up a chair.

"Unpacked and everything," said Enid. "I really appreciate you guys helping with my trunk."

"Best way to meet the freshmen girls, right James?" said Dennis.

"Hey, our motives were strictly altruistic," said the other boy. He smiled at me and it was as if for the first time he snapped into focus. He wasn't in the background anymore, but had moved to the center of the picture, a skinny boy with blondish hair and gray eyes fringed with dark lashes. I was surprised I hadn't noticed before how attractive he was. He had that tawny skin with a faint olive undertone that never burns in the sun. I would have loved to make him smile again, but I was half afraid to speak.

"I'm James Stuart," he said. "Dennis and I are the dorm advisors at Coolidge."

I mumbled my name. I had to remind myself firmly that Dusty would never be rattled just because a boy smiled at her.

At the other end of the table Carol and her fiancé, Paul Alexi were getting into a political argument with a couple of guys whose names I didn't catch. Next to me, Dennis leaned attentively toward Enid, obviously already bent on building something rich and beautiful between them. That left James and me. I was overwhelmed with longing for the days in high school when I had shyly buried my nose in a paperback book at lunch. A girl like Dusty would never think of hiding behind a paperback. She was comfortable with boys, I reminded myself. Even boys she found attractive.

"Where are you from?" I choked out. I was relieved that my voice sounded relatively normal. Maybe this would be easier than I thought.

"I'm from St. Pete," he said.

That was a surprise. Somehow I had imagined he must come from someplace far away, someplace exotic. "You mean you're from right here in town? Goodness, why don't you live at home and just commute?"

"Would *you* live at home and commute if you could?" he asked.

That stopped me short. "I see what you mean. I guess I wouldn't. Are you a senior, like Dennis?" I asked.

"No, I'm a sophomore."

"And you're a dorm advisor?"

He shrugged. "Well, Dennis swore to me that it wasn't very hard and it brings it a few extra bucks so I signed up."

"What do dorm advisors have to do?" It had suddenly occurred to me that if it brought in a few extra bucks I might apply to do it myself.

"Mostly you hold the hands of the nervous freshmen, answer their questions, try to spot if anybody's going out of their minds. Not that it happens that often, but we did have something like that last year. It was a guy in my class, as a matter of fact, awful good-looking guy, but bats. He was out on the fill making out with this freshman girl and suddenly he says to her, 'I've always wanted to kill something beautiful.' "

I gasped.

James smiled. "Don't worry. She ran screaming to the campus cops. The poor guy was carried off campus in a strait-jacket. I saw them driving away, with Dr. Philpot, the school psychologist, in the car and I swear Philpot looked worse than the crazy guy. When he signed on as campus psychologist, I don't think he figured he'd be getting into anything as heavy as that."

"Gee!"

James looked amused. "You're really into clean language, huh? I don't think I've heard anybody say 'gee' since the fourth grade." He proceeded to give some examples of things people did say.

"I'm very wholesome," I said, embarrassed.

"Hey, cut it out down there," said Paul. "You corrupting Carol's freshmen already?"

"Come on, Alexi, look who's talking."

Suddenly, I wasn't very hungry, so I grabbed the opportunity to get up and dump my tray. On the way back to the table, I stopped at the coffee urn and got myself a cup of coffee. My heart was thumping wildly. I wasn't sure whether it was the lurid story about the incident on the fill, or James's bad language. Just possibly it was his gray eyes. I was pleased that I had been able to engage in a natural-sounding conversation with him, but there was no use trying to tell myself that I was perfectly comfortable.

When I got back to the table, James was looking

a little sheepish. "I thought maybe you'd gone off," he said. "Like maybe I offended you or something."

From this I deduced that his salty language was not quite so typical of college life as he had led me to believe. This was the sort of thing I had to pay attention to. College seemed so different that I felt as if I were studying the customs of some primitive Polynesian tribe. I didn't want to make any wrong moves.

I gulped. "I just went to get coffee. I was very interested in what you were saying about being a dorm advisor." Particularly the part about it being a paid position, I thought as I sat down.

"Yeah, well, the only time things get a little tricky is when you've got to play the bad guy and enforce law and order. You know, when somebody's music is too loud or they're otherwise making a pig of themselves in some major way. Believe me, I'm not one to sweat the small stuff, but every now and then you can't let things go by. Like last year, this guy in my dorm came in drunk, threw a brick through that window over there. Then he started going through the halls at Coolidge with this stripper he had picked up downtown. He was swinging a champagne bottle and singing *Waltzing Matilda* at two in the morning."

"We can't have that kind of noise," Dennis said solemnly.

"Right. Besides, there was the window. That's the kind of thing the administration expects us to clamp down on. And Dennis goes home on weekends, so if anything like that happens this year, I guess coping with it is going to fall pretty much on me."

I couldn't stop thinking about the crazy guy on

the fill. "What ever happened to that poor girl who almost got killed?" I inquired.

"What? Oh, you mean Marsha." He grinned. "Well, I do hear she hasn't been out on the fill since."

I shivered a little. I hoped my freshman year wasn't going to include the experience of somebody trying to murder me. Even Dusty might have trouble handling something like that. "Where is the fill, by the way?" I asked. My plan was to avoid it.

"Out by the sea wall." He twisted around in his seat. "Well, you can't see it from here, but when you go back to your complex you can probably see the dredging equipment still working out there. It spits up sand from the bottom and they keep piling the sand up and piling it up until they've got new waterfront land. That's what attracts all the gulls. When the equipment throws that sand up it's full of shellfish and things, kind of a cafeteria for gulls. Anyway, the land they make that way is called fill. But you can't build on it right away because it's got to settle in. If you walk out there now, in some places you sink practically to your knees. So it's kind of deserted out there. Lots of privacy."

"Don't you believe it," snorted Carol. "I can look out my window any Saturday morning and see somebody or another dragging a blanket back from out near the sea wall. Some nights it practically rates as densely inhabited."

"She exaggerates," said James, smiling at me. "There are miles of sea wall. Plenty of room for all of us."

This was the kind of talk which in high school would have embarrassed me. Now, however, I was steadied by remembering that Dusty was used to boys and the kind of things they say. She was the sort of person, I was sure, who would just laugh at a remark like that. I couldn't quite manage a laugh, but I did achieve what I hoped was a vaguely cheerful expression.

"How did you ever get a name like Dusty?" James asked suddenly.

I choked on my coffee and reached hastily for my napkin. When I finally got my breath, I said, "Oh, I don't know. How does anybody get a nickname?"

"Search me," said James. "Nobody's ever dared to give me a nickname. I'd whop 'em alongside-a duh head."

"Me either," Dennis chimed in. "I've broken off with girls for less serious offenses than calling me Denny."

"I've never had a nickname either," said Carol.

"Hey, wait a minute," protested Paul. "What about how I call you Sugar Butt?"

In the resulting hilarity, everyone forgot all about my nickname. But I knew I was going to have to construct a good cover story before the subject came up again.

Chapter Three

I was already wondering when I would see James Stuart again. I had begun daydreaming of that fleeting smile of his. But I had other things on my mind, too. I had to find my way to all my classes. Luckily, the administration had given each of us a map of the campus, which was a help. When I got to Core Science, freshmen were already streaming into the tiered seats. The preppie girls, Mandy and Cindy, waved at me from the top row. I decided to sit on the bottom row, as far away from them as possible.

It took me a while to figure out how to pull up the seat's extra arm which provided a small writing surface on which to take notes. Glancing over my shoulder, I saw that Cindy and Mandy already had theirs in place. Perhaps I should have gone up to sit by them after all. They must be smarter than they looked. I finally got the thing locked in place just as the professor came in. He was a skinny man with very short gray hair and brown age spots on his face and hands.

"I am Professor Reed," he said. He began tossing a piece of chalk into the air with one hand. "And this is Core Science. Is everyone in the right place?"

He cast an eye over the room full of freshmen. He wore rimless glasses low on his nose and when he spoke to us he looked over them rather than through them, which gave him an intimidating air of superiority. In spite of the coldness of his blue eyes, no one actually bolted out of the room.

In a quick, nervous voice, Professor Reed launched into a history of scientific inquiry. As he spoke, centuries and decades of scientific advances whizzed by. I wrote frantically, trying to get it all down. After some forty minutes, he began winding up with a brief glance at recent research. My fingers were numb. DNA, RNA, messenger RNA, transfer RNA, amino acids, and proteins spun by. I was past worrying about how everything fit together. I was just hoping to get it all down so I could figure it out later. Finally, he dropped the chalk he had been tossing and dusted his hands off. He was finished. I slumped in my seat.

A minute later we were filing out into the bright sunshine. The callus on the side of the middle finger on my right hand was indented from the pressure of my ballpoint. I flexed my finger carefully. If this was the introductory lecture, I thought, what was the rest of the course going to be like?

Even though I was on a strict budget, I felt that I deserved a cup of coffee. Maybe caffeine would help restore me. I headed toward the student union.

A jukebox was playing inside the union and two boys were doing a passable imitation of a bullfight in time to the music. One of the them had taken off his shirt and was holding it out like a matador's cape. A loose-limbed blond guy was playing at being the bull. He kept lowering his head and rushing at the shirt, his index fingers held up against his head as horns. In the booths lining the room people sat placidly drinking coffee. No one seemed to notice the mock bullfight. I deduced that it was the custom in college to ignore weirdness. My coffee cost fifty cents, which was enough to deter me from getting a Danish. I tucked my notebook under one arm and made my way to a booth, taking care to steer clear of the bullfight.

When I sat down, I saw why the interior of the union seemed dim. The glass in the windows had been tinted sepia, the brown color of old photographs. From my booth, I could see kids outside passing by on the sidewalk, some passing only inches away from me. Through the tinted glass they looked better defined than they had in the glaring sun outside. A girl walked by in a blue skirt gathered at the hip, her loose T-shirt fashionably wrinkled. I saw a couple of people that I figured must be Founding Freshmen. They seemed to have that indefinable air of looniness Carol had described. I saw one boy dressed in new clothes straight out of the L.L. Bean catalog. The usual assortment of jeans and disheveled hair passed by, plus some out-of-it looks and one or two clean-cut types with eager faces. I wondered how many of these kids were acting out a new college identity as I was.

Suddenly, a familiar figure appeared. I would know that rosy cheeked, blank face anywhere. It was Margaret Wentworth, the Presbyterian minister's daughter. My reflective mood vanished to be replaced by panic. I quickly turned my back to the window and buried my nose in my notebook. I could just imagine her careening into the union and shrieking, "Deborah Susan, *what* have you done to your *hair?*"

But to my relief she didn't seem to be coming into the union. She was passing by. And, I reminded myself, she would never connect the back of a platinum blond head with me. I was safe. I should review my Core Science notes, I told myself. That would calm me. I wiped my sweaty palms on my jeans and stared at my notes. The *Guide to Success in College* had explained that going over your notes after every class was the key to success.

"Studying already?"

I looked up to see James Stuart looming over me. He was holding a cup of coffee and a Danish. His gray eyes were shadowed in the dim light and I couldn't quite make out his expression. I hoped it was friendly.

I blinked. "I thought I'd better review my notes. That first lecture in Core Science was scary. I took a lot of science in high school but it was all I could do to keep up with what he was saying. I mean, he's practically covered the breadth of scientific knowledge in the first lecture. What's he going to do for an encore?"

He slid in the booth. "Don't worry about it. You'll have a couple of more lectures like that one, survey things, then you'll start doing some lab work."

He propped one foot up next to me. Eyeing his battered tennis shoes, I was painfully aware of his closeness. "Lab work?" I said weakly. I was already regretting that in high school I had let my lab partner dissect the fetal pig while I cravenly confined myself to taking notes. "We didn't have the most up–to–date lab facilities in Ocala. I just don't have heaps of experience."

"No problem. Chances are that in Reed's unit your lab work will be out in the bay. Reed is the world expert on barnacles. Didn't you know? Before long, you'll be wading out there counting barnacles on dock pilings. Absolutely the only skill necessary is a certain imperviousness to saltwater and an ability to count." He bit into his Danish. "Don't worry so much."

I was stung. Deborah Susan might worry, but Dusty never did. Never.

I tossed my notebook aside carelessly. "I wasn't worried," I said. "I make it a point not to worry. I just take each day as it comes." I beamed a confident smile at him but it was wasted because he didn't even look up. He was staring into his coffee cup.

"I guess you know Enid and Dennis went out together last night," he said.

I nodded. "Enid said they took a long walk and then popped into Lou's for a late night snack."

"Another good man bites the dust."

"Hey, all they did was take a walk."

"A *long* walk," he said. "Believe me, I know the signs."

"What's so bad about Dennis and Enid going out together anyway?"

"You'll see. You've never lost a friend this way, I can tell. When a person gets to be part of a couple, everything changes. Suddenly *phht*—they don't have any time for you any more."

"Hey, guys!" Enid waved. She and Dennis were bearing down on us, carrying cups of coffee.

We slid over to make room for them when they sat down. I looked at their expressions closely but could not see any sign that they were embarking on some hot romance. Not that it was exactly easy to read Dennis. His mouth was a long, patient line that didn't give much away.

"Who do you have for Western Civ., Dusty?" Enid asked. "I've got Carter."

I pulled my schedule out of my purse and checked it. "Stuart," I said. James had draped a napkin over his head. I decided to ignore it, following the rule I had just observed—that the cool college student ignores weirdness. "Have you had Core Science yet?"

"This afternoon."

"Well, brace yourself," I said. "The opening lecture is fairly intimidating."

"I'm not worried about science," said Enid. "What I'm worried about is Western Civ. Did you get started on that reading list they sent us this summer?"

I hesitated. Something told me that Dusty would not have touched her reading list during the summer. She would have been too busy hanging out with her many friends. "I made a start on it," I hedged. Actually, I had read about half of them.

"I think the list must be somebody's idea of humor. Plato's *Republic?* This is where we *start?* I may kill myself," said Enid, lighting up a cigarette.

"If you keep that up," said Dennis, looking at her, "you just might."

"I know, I know, but when I'm jumpy, I have to have one," she said. "If I could just totally eliminate stress from my life, I'd kick the habit in a minute."

I dabbed at my eyes with a napkin.

"Ooops," said Enid remorsefully. "I forgot that smoke bothers Dusty's contacts." She stubbed the cigarette out in the glass ashtray on the table.

I laid my napkin over the ashtray in an effort to contain the last wisps of smoke.

I couldn't wait to get Enid back at the dorm alone and probe what was going on between her and Dennis. I also wanted to find out what Enid thought about James. I would have to be careful how I went at this since, unlike Deborah Susan, Dusty was supposed to know all about boys. My best friends were boys—wasn't that what I had said to Enid? It was just possible that I had laid that on a trifle too thick. It looked as if Enid was the one with all the experience with boys. I wished I could just lay out all my insecurities and ignorance before her and ask for advice. But I had burned that bridge behind me when I decided to become Dusty.

"Could I squeeze in with you?" It was Ann, the girl with the chic clothes and the freckles.

"Sure," I said. Enid was so small there was plenty of room on our side.

"Don't let me eat all of this," said Ann. She stuck her spoon into her ice cream sundae. "When I get halfway through, stop me. Tie me to the chair if you have to. I mean it. Wasn't that lecture of Reed's awful?"

"Were you there? I didn't see you," I said.

"I was cringing in my seat. The public schools of Skinner's Hollow, Kentucky, are not exactly strong in the sciences. I mean, I was but totally lost in there. Do you mind if I look over your notes some,

35

Dusty? I saw you were in there scribbling like a madman."

For a split second, it did not register that she was asking me a question. I had not quite got used to answering to the name of Dusty. "Uh, sure," I said.

"Oh, forget I said anything," she said ruefully. "Sooner or later I've got to learn to take my own notes. I guess I ought to start now."

"No, really, that would be fine if you looked at mine. Maybe I'll look at yours, too. Maybe you got some things I missed."

"My notes are pathetic, I promise you. But if you wouldn't mind letting me see yours just this once, maybe by next time I'll have recovered from the shock of it all and can do better."

"Eeek, look at the time," I said. "I've got Western Civ. and I don't even know where it is."

"Oh, gosh me, too," said Enid.

"Everybody has Western Civ. at the same time," Dennis pointed out mildly.

"Yikes, you mean, that means me, too?" said Ann, groping for her schedule. "Oh, dear, that means I'm not going to be able to eat this sundae after all. Maybe it's a blessing in disguise. I ought to save my calories for the get-acquainted luau tonight. When I think of all the calories in roast suckling pig, it makes me ill."

Ann and I both had Stuart for Western Civ., so we went together to look for the classroom. Other freshmen were straggling in when we got there. We took seats in the circle of desks that had been arranged at the front of the room and eyed each other apprehensively.

A few minutes later, Professor Stuart arrived. My

first impression of him was not reassuring. He looked like one of those Medicis who wore poison rings back in the Renaissance, dark with a bent nose that almost touched his lips, brown, hooded eyes and sallow skin. But to my surprise, when he spoke, his voice was gentle. And he certainly didn't dress like any sinister Medici prince. He was wearing baggy pants and a frayed knit shirt with an alligator on the pocket. He called roll and handed out thick packets of discussion guides. I promised myself that I would curl up with Plato and the study guide at the nearest opportunity. I wasn't sure whether they would take away my scholarship money if my grades weren't up to par, but I didn't want to tempt them.

Professor Stuart gave us a little talk designed to convince us that, properly understood, *The Republic* was more exciting than a rock video. Then he let us go early.

As soon as we got outside, Ann said, "This sophomore I talked to at breakfast said you don't really have to read all the books in Western Civ. as long as you grasp the concepts. What do you think?"

"I'd be afraid to try it," I said. Then I remembered that Dusty was not the worrying type. I was going to have to erase the word 'afraid' from my vocabulary. "I don't mean literally 'afraid'," I went on quickly. "I just mean skipping the reading is okay for those who want to, but the way I look at it. We're here to get an education, right? For all we know, Plato might be fascinating the way the man says. Besides, think what it would be like to sit around during discussion group trying to cover up that you hadn't read the stuff."

I heard the words come out of my mouth with a critical and doubting ear. Somehow what I had said didn't sound quite like Dusty. I wasn't always sure what she would say. During all those hours I had spent at Burger King during the summer imagining her, I hadn't once pictured her reading Plato.

Chapter Four

When I came in from my calculus class that afternoon, men on tall ladders were stringing lights in the trees in front of the cafeteria and long tables covered with white tablecloths had been brought out onto the lawn. Near the tables someone in a chef's hat was prodding the coals under a roasting pig. I ran upstairs to my room and found Enid in the process of slipping into a flowered halter top.

"What do you think?" she asked. "Does this look Hawaiian? What I really need is a grass skirt, but my green wrap-around is going to have to do." She stepped into leather thongs which were maybe a size four. Thumbelina could have worn Enid's shoes.

Strains of music were coming from outside. "Do you think everybody is going to dress Hawaiian?"

"Oh, I doubt it. Can you picture Dennis in a flowered shirt?"

My problem, I realized, was that I was not sure which I was more afraid of—looking out of it, or looking ridiculous. If I had been only worried about looking out of it, I could have improvised a sarong from a sheet and painted it over with Magic Marker flowers. But I was too afraid of looking ridiculous.

I took a quick breath and reminded myself of how happy-go-lucky Dusty was. She was not the sort of person to worry about what she wore because what she wore was, *by definition,* the right thing to wear.

Providentially, at that moment, as I thumbed through my dresser drawers the perfect Dusty-type T-shirt surfaced. I had bought it just before leaving for school. "I'm a Party Animal," it said.

After I slipped into it I began to feel better. "Enid, you know James Stuart?"

"Mmm," she said.

"Well, what do you think of him? He's kind of an unusual type, wouldn't you say?"

"I think I'd better touch up the polish on my toenails," she said absently. "James? I like him. He and Dennis are really close friends."

"But it's kind of hard to tell what kind of person he is, don't you think?"

"Naturally, it takes a while to really get to know somebody," Enid said placidly.

What I really wanted to know was whether Enid had seen any signs that James might be interested in me, but I didn't like to ask her outright.

"I get the idea he's really not the type to settle down with one girl. You know, just breezy and friendly to everybody." I added hastily. "And I think he's absolutely right about that. College is a time for really enjoying your independence, trying out lots of different things, getting to know lots of different kinds of people. I personally wouldn't want to get paired off at this point in the game."

Enid smiled a faraway smile. "Everybody feels like that until she finds the right person, Dusty. Like with Dennis and me. We both had played the field, but almost the minute we met each other, that was all over. We had this instant rapport, you know? A closeness. We can talk to each other about absolutely anything."

I brooded about that a minute while I tied my tennis shoes. I certainly didn't feel I could talk to James about anything. In fact, I could hardly say hello to him without getting breathless. I thought about how lovely it would be to have instant rapport instead of this uncomfortable pounding of the heart.

Ann stuck her red head in our door. "Are you all just about ready to go?"

"Just about," said Enid. "Let's go down together. Is Meg ready, too?"

"I think she must have already gone down," Ann said.

We spotted Meg as soon as we approached the tables. She was sipping from a straw stuck into a coconut and looking under her lashes at a good-looking brunette boy across the table. We waved at her but she did not seem to see us.

Just then my science professor, Professor Reed, passed by with a hibiscus behind one ear.

A cafeteria employee was going down the line giving out paper leis. I draped a pink one and a green one around my neck. Over by the cafeteria, I saw Professor Stuart trying to light his pipe. He was cupping his hand around it, trying to protect his match from the breeze coming off the bay.

James and Dennis materialized beside us. "You're a party animal?" James said, looking at my shirt.

I looked down at it, suddenly self-conscious. "It was marked down."

"No, I like it. Don't you like it, Dennis?"

Dennis looked at it soberly for a moment. "Very nice."

"Let's get some food now," said Enid. "Before the shrimp are gone."

There it was again, I thought, ruefully, that pounding of the heart. I hoped my face was not turning pink. We filled our plates and began looking for a place to sit down.

"I think there's room for us all over there," said Enid.

To my horror, I saw that at the table she was pointing to, Margaret Wentworth was engaged in earnest conversation with a girl I didn't know.

"What about over there?" I said, waving my hand wildly in the opposite direction.

"We'd be downwind from the pig there," Enid pointed out.

"All the more atmosphere," said James.

"But what about all that smoke and Dusty's contacts?"

I did not care where we sat so long as I avoided Margaret Wentworth. I suddenly pulled out a chair that was right in front of me. "How about right here?"

"But there aren't enough seats together here," said Enid.

"Don't worry about me," said Ann wanly. "I'll find someplace else to sit."

"You want us to move over a couple of seats so you all can sit together?" suggested a boy sitting at the table.

I was so relieved I felt like falling on his neck with kisses but I didn't want to do anything to call attention to myself with Margaret so near. The boy and his friends scooted over. I sat down with my back to Margaret and at once felt much better.

But as we ate, I kept casting surreptitious glances in Margaret's direction. Her table was filling up with kids and they all looked like Margaret— incredibly clean and earnest.

"Why do I feel my brilliant table talk fails to keep your attention?" said James. "What is so fascinating about the God Squad over there?"

"The God Squad?"

"The bunch over by the tree. Marion Henderson et al."

"Oh, is that what they're called? The God Squad? I was just thinking they all look alike."

James looked in their direction critically. "They do. It's that scrubbed-behind-the-ears look. But they don't look more alike than any other bunch on campus, do you think, Dennis?"

"What?" said Dennis, reluctantly tearing his attention away from Enid.

James shot me a meaningful look and repeated patiently, "I don't think the God Squad look any more alike than any other group on campus, do you?"

"Cleaner," suggested Dennis.

James was sitting next to Ann instead of next to me. While this made it easier for me to breathe, I could not help wondering if he had maybe noticed that I found him attractive and was deliberately putting distance between us to discourage me. It was a mortifying thought.

"What would you say are the groups on campus, James?" Ann asked.

"Look over there," said James, gesturing to a barefoot boy in stonewashed, ragged jeans and unkempt hair who was carrying a pineapple under one arm. "That's one of the weirdos, also known as the granola bunch. They're the ones who remember the sixties and keep it holy. Drugs and paisley bedspreads are the rule with that bunch. Now by way of contrast, catch the girl by that pyramid of coconuts—a classic preppie type. The preppies wash and blow dry their hair every morning and after college they go into investment banking or start their own accounting firms. Money is to the preppie what drugs are to the granola bunch."

A blond guy with a deep tan strode by us. He had a long face, wore glasses and looked serious even in a lei, no easy thing.

"What about him?" Ann said. "Where does he fit in?"

"That's Jim Waters, a veteran going to school on the G.I. bill. The vets don't exactly fit in any group, but the girls are crazy about them."

Ann looked down quickly and busied herself with her sweet and sour pork. "How can you tell all these things just by looking at people?" she asked.

"I can't. I make it all up."

"Seriously," she said, "do you think you can really tell what kind of person somebody is just by the way he looks?"

"I'm afraid so," he said.

"Oh, no you can't," I said. "All you can tell from the way people look is what they want you to think.

There's no reason why a future investment banker couldn't hide away in dirty jeans."

"Never happen," said James.

"How do you know? I think it does. Some of the time, anyway."

"Okay, but you know what would happen if a potential investment banker dressed like a weirdo? He would turn into a weirdo, that's what. He'd run around with a lot of other weirdos and end up frying his brain on drugs and the next thing you know he's handing out flowers in the airport and saying, 'What's happening, man?' "

"You must think clothes are amazingly powerful."

"You must think people are naturally deceitful," he countered.

I shot him a quick look, suddenly aware that I had said too much.

"Okay," said James. "Let's study this question objectively. Look at Dusty here."

He reached over the table and touched my hair. I felt my face growing warm.

He looked at me critically. "Blondes have more fun, hey?" he said. "So that's the message with the hair. And our next exhibit is the T-shirt. 'I'm a Party Animal.' "

"Cut it out, James," said Dennis. "You're embarrassing her."

"I'm just making a point. Dusty understands me perfectly. So do we look at Dusty and conclude that under this party animal disguise lives the soul of a serious scholar?"

"I might surprise you," I said tartly.

He grinned. "You won't surprise me."

For an uncomfortable moment there I had the feeling he was reading my SAT scores off my forehead.

"Come on, quit picking on the girl," Dennis said. "Or I'll have to come around there and wring your worthless neck."

"Yes, leave her alone, James," said Enid. "Dusty just dresses that way because she's not into material things. She doesn't want to get caught up in superficialities and I think that's great. She's antimaterialistic."

"Now don't start analyzing *my* clothes," Ann said hastily. "I'm not ready to be typecast."

"Oh, come on," said James. "You're seventeen years old. You mean to tell me you don't have any idea yet what kind of person you are?"

Ann turned beet red, a color that clashed painfully with her carrot-colored hair.

"You know but you aren't telling?" said James. "Okay, let's look at your clothes."

"I don't know this guy," said Dennis.

"Not off the rack in our mass market stores," said James, squinting at Ann's clothes. "Not scooped up out of a drugstore bin like Dusty's nonmaterialistic shirt. Say, you don't happen to buy your clothes in New York, do you?"

"You are spooky," said Ann respectfully.

"Merely observant. Now your accent says Kentucky or Tennessee but your clothes are upscale New York. I think your clothes reveal a certain sophistication."

Ann blushed. "So what else do you see in your crystal ball?"

He threw up his hands. "The swami is out to lunch. I quit."

I was annoyed. Maybe as much as anything I was annoyed at myself for being so susceptible to James. If there was one thing I was sure of about Dusty it was that she didn't melt into a simpering puddle the first time an attractive boy was the least bit friendly to her. She could take them or leave them.

"Okay, now it's my turn," I said firmly. "Let's take James here, folks." I leaned over the table and plucked at his shirt. "Coldly observant to a fault, for tact count zero. He's clever but with uncertain or negligible loyalty to others. I think we've got here the makings of a CIA operative or possibly a future sociologist."

"Hey!" protested Enid. "I don't know if I like that, Dusty. I'm thinking of being a sociologist myself."

James looked at me indulgently. "You haven't mentioned my clothes yet."

"That's because I think you can tell a lot more about a person by what comes out of his mouth."

Dennis looked amused. "Here's one you don't intimidate, James."

"Hey, I welcome worthy adversaries. Always. Especially blond party animals."

After dinner, as we were walking back to the dorm, Ann said, "That James Stuart is something else. I'm surprised you didn't hit him, Dusty."

"He doesn't bother me."

"I think he likes you," said Enid.

"Why do you say that?" My voice sounded muffled to my own ears.

"Oh, just the way he's always looking at you. I think he's intrigued."

"You know, he wasn't a hundred percent right about my clothes," Ann said diffidently. "I have bought one or two things in New York, but I make most of my clothes."

I stopped in my tracks. "You should have told him that!"

"I didn't want to advertise it. You know, people don't respect your clothes when they find out you make them yourself. Haven't you ever heard somebody say 'And she makes her own clothes' and then everybody laughs."

I had to admit that she had a point.

I had succeeded in avoiding Margaret Wentworth at the luau but I should have known I couldn't keep it up forever. Later that night I was in my bathrobe, brushing my teeth when all of a sudden I came face to face with her.

Margaret's flaxed hair was wrapped over pink plastic curlers, and her blue eyes were bulging.

I choked on my toothpaste.

"Deborah Susan?" she said hesitantly. "I thought that looked like you, but *what* have you *done* to your *hair?* Are you all right? You aren't choking or anything are you?"

I spit the toothpaste out in the sink and tried to catch my breath before straightening up.

"Are you okay?" she repeated. "Because I know how to do the Heimlich maneuver, if you aren't."

I straightened up at once. The last thing I wanted was to have Margaret bending me over a sink and pounding me on the back. It was exactly the sort of thing she would do, too.

"I was just a little bit startled," I said, with what dignity I could muster. I wiped the toothpaste off the corners of my mouth with the back of my hand. I couldn't think when I'd last seen someone in pink curlers, but that was Margaret all over, old fashioned to the core. "Look, Margaret, everybody here calls me Dusty. And I'd like you to, too."

"I don't know if I can remember," she said. "Why did you bleach your hair and cut it all off? You had such pretty hair."

"I like it better this way. And you won't forget I'm called Dusty, will you?"

"It's just going to be so hard for me to remember. Why do you want to be called Dusty? Deborah Susan is such a pretty name."

I took a deep breath. "Dusty is what my grandfather called me, and it was his dying wish that I call myself that when I went away to college."

"Oh. Well, I'll try to remember, but I'm just so used to calling you Deborah Susan, it's going to be hard."

"Please work on it. What are you doing here, anyway?"

"Well, it's a good school, and not so far from home that I'd have to pay plane fare, and I'm really interested in the religion major. A lot of schools don't offer that."

"I didn't mean that. I mean what are you doing in this bathroom?"

"I just came in to brush my teeth."

"You mean you *live* here?" It was worse than I thought.

"I live on the ground floor, actually. But a bunch of people were washing out panty hose in the sinks down there so I came on upstairs. I like to get to bed early. Isn't it nice us running into each other this way? I didn't know there was anybody else from Ocala here. Why didn't you tell me that you were going to Blake?"

"I made up my mind at the last minute." I held my toothbrush under the running water for a moment and turned to go. "You'll remember what I said about my name, won't you?"

"Dusty," she repeated obediently.

"Right."

I had almost gotten to the door when she said, "Wait a minute, Deborah Susan, I mean Dusty. Gee, that sounds awful funny."

"You'll get used to it."

"Look, I wonder if you'd be interested in joining this weekly prayer group some of us are getting together on the ground floor. Nothing formal, just a time of quiet communion every Wednesday night. Sort of a time out from the stresses and strains of college life to get back in touch with what really matters."

"Thank you. But I'm thinking of converting to Buddhism."

"Well, if you change your mind . . ."

I hurried away. Margaret Wentworth actually living in my dorm! How could this happen to me?

When I got back to my room, I felt weak at the knees, but Enid didn't notice that anything was wrong. "Oh, good, you're back," she said. "Ann was just here. She got a huge care package of brownies from home and she's inviting a bunch of us in to help her eat them so she won't be tempted to eat them all herself."

I wondered if Margaret had also been invited to share the brownies. No, she couldn't have been. How many brownies could come by parcel post anyway?

We trudged over to Ann's room. "Oh, good," Ann said when we walked in. Her mouth was full. "I saved you some." She held out the box.

Meg, her long hair hiding half her face, was perched on top of her desk. She was dressed in a filmy peignoir, and was talking to an assortment of upperclassmen sprawled around the room. Our entrance scarcely caused her to miss a beat.

"So then he said he was married," she said, smiling. "And I said, 'That just makes you more fascinating.' " She tossed her long hair back but it immediately swung back in front of her face. "And he was absolutely horrified. He said, 'How can you go out with a married man?' "

"Maybe he was trying to get rid of you," I said, "and was surprised that you couldn't take a hint."

She gave me a slow look. "It wasn't like that. He was very much in love with me. He was just a very sweet, very old fashioned——."

"Adulterer," said Ann. She covered her mouth. "Ooops, that just popped out."

"Well, if you want to be *medieval* about it," said Meg.

The girl sitting cross-legged at the foot of Ann's bed had short hair and a boyish figure. "Laurie" was embroidered on the pocket of her nightshirt. "I don't like older men," she said. "They're so moldy. All that hair on their chests."

51

"Laurie likes Brandon," said a girl with plump arms. She was pulling a brush through her long black hair.

"Do you mean Brandon Farrow?" said Meg. "Oh, I've met him."

Laurie shot her an alarmed look.

"He came up to me at the luau," Meg went on in her soft voice, "and said, 'You look to me as if you have a secret.' I just laughed a little because I like to think that I *might* have a secret."

"Brandon comes on to everybody," said a buxom girl in a long T-shirt. "He's a positive hazard."

"Do you think so?" said Meg, parting her hair with her hands so she could peek through it. "I thought he seemed very, very sweet. I thought we might have something really special together."

Everyone seemed to be looking at Laurie.

"Hey, guys, I don't own Brandon," Laurie protested. "It's a free country."

"These are really great brownies," I told Ann.

"My mother is a fantastic cook," she said. "This is her secret double chocolate recipe."

But my efforts to stem the tide of the conversation were futile. The talk veered back to boys and stayed there, the girl with the plump arms contributing some reminiscences that were astounding if true.

After a while, I explained that I had an eight o'clock class and excused myself.

I had to brush my teeth again since I had eaten the brownie, and when I finally got back to the room, Enid was getting into bed. "Something about that Meg gets on my nerves," she said, putting her glasses on the desk near her bed. "I don't know what it is."

"She's always smiling, for one thing."

"Do you think she was making all that junk up?"

I hadn't thought of that. "You know, that is very possible."

I got in bed and pulled the covers up to my chin. I loved the mattress. It was heaven compared to the one at home, which had a broken spring that skewered me in the hip every time I rolled over. Drowsily, I wondered if there weren't a niche some place between the wild sex bunch and the prayer group bunch where a wholesome, laid-back, peroxide blond could exist in tolerable comfort.

"I feel sorry for Ann," Enid said. "Having to live with Meg every day."

"Mmm," I said. It was funny how often I thought of James when I was falling asleep. I could count on it, when I was hovering at the edge of consciousness—an image of his honey-colored skin and his dark lashes and gray eyes swam in my mind. Maybe Dusty could take them or leave them, but Deborah Susan was another matter. Enid thought James was interested in me, and she seemed to know a lot about boys. Could she be right?

The next day, I went by the campus mail room and learned that I, too, had received a care package, just like Anne. Well, not *exactly* like Anne. Instead of double chocolate brownies, my mother had sent a box packed with dried skim milk, a packet of raisins and Econo-Brand cookies, half of them now crumbling in their cellophane wrapping. It was incredible how much that pathetic care package reminded me of home. It was like when that famous

French writer tasted a bit of delicate madeleine pastry and suddenly had a flashback to his childhood. When I looked at those stale Econo-Brand cookies, I could almost hear the blare of the television in my family's living room. As if the package were poison, I hastily dropped it into the nearest wastebasket.

Chapter Five

I spent most of the next weekend holed up in my room working on my first Western Civ. paper. The topic was Plato's idea of justice. It was not something I could dash off from the top of my head.

"Let's get out of this room," Enid said finally. "I'm going to go bonkers if I don't get out."

I had to agree that it was time for a break.

It was a soft and starry night and we didn't have far to walk to the student union. My shoulders were a mass of cramped muscles after all my hours bent over the typewriter and I shrugged and swung my arms to loosen them up. "Dennis isn't around tonight?" I asked. Lately, I had noticed, he always seemed to be around.

"He goes home for the weekends."

"Oh, right, I forgot."

"Do you know his parents had to sell their house to pay for Roger's defense? He was up for four counts of capital murder, and they got the best lawyer in the state hoping to get a reduced charge. You can imagine what it cost. Dennis says his parents have aged tremendously since it happened. All he thinks about is that he doesn't want to do anything that would make it worse for them because they've already had so much trouble. I think they really kind of lean on him. He's had to grow up fast." She sighed. "It's tough."

We pushed open the heavy glass door of the union.

"I think I'll go wash my hands," I said.

"I'll wait for you."

"No, you go ahead," I said. "I'll meet you at the booth."

In the bathroom, I scrubbed my hands until I was reasonably sure Enid had gotten her order. Then I quit doing the lady Macbeth number, went on up to the grill and ordered a cup of hot water.

"Hot water?" said the guy in the apron. "That's all? I don't know what I should charge you for that."

"How about a nickel?" I suggested hopefully.

"Let's make it a dime." He tossed my dime in the open drawer of the cash register.

I dropped the tea bag I had saved from dinner into the cup of hot water and made my way toward the booths in the next room. I could tell right away where Enid was sitting by the cloud of smoke rising from the booth in the corner. She was puffing hard trying to get in her quota of nicotine before I arrived.

When I reached the booth, she stubbed out her cigarette and waved at the smoke ineffectually with her hands. A guy I didn't recognize was sitting across from her. "Dusty, do you know Rice?" she asked.

Rice MacEnroe was wearing shorts. The leg that he had thrown carelessly out from the booth was muscular and covered with curly black hair. He had a large, heavy looking head, untidy dark hair and a five-o'clock shadow. He gazed at me with melancholy, basset-hound eyes and I returned his look. It was mutual dislike at first sight. "Hullo, Dusty," he said. He had a very deep voice, basso profundo.

I nodded a perfunctory greeting and sat down beside Enid. I certainly wasn't going to sit down next to Rice.

"Rice is from Miami," Enid said.

My parents, in their small town provincial way, had always regarded Miami as a hotbed of vice, crime, and transplanted New Yorkers. I could not help remembering all of this when I looked at Rice. Particularly the vice and crime part.

"I was just telling Enid that you can't even get a decent margarita in this hick town," he said.

I regarded him suspiciously over the rim of my tea cup.

"Not that I care," he went on. "I have to be hitting the books all the time. I'm pre-med."

He paused, evidently expecting us to genuflect.

Then he held out his hands and flexed the fingers, staring broodingly at them with his dark eyes. I had to admit his hands were arresting in appearance. They looked as if they must weigh several pounds each. "These hands," he said in a low voice. "Can you believe these are a surgeon's hands?"

I couldn't, as a matter of fact. I also couldn't believe how phony he was.

"I suppose pre-med is really tough, huh?" said Enid.

He shrugged and looked off into the distance. "I can handle it," he said. "The only thing is, I need to

57

get away some to myself. To think. To be alone. I can't believe they won't let freshmen have cars out here. And nothing for miles around but that tacky food joint across the highway." He muttered something else under his breath, but the only words I made out were "stir-crazy."

"Rice, dar-ling," drawled a female voice. "I've locked myself out of my car again. Is that grim or what?"

Rice slowly rose and I saw that he was not tall, no taller, in fact, than the girl who had approached our booth. She was wearing a matching cotton sweater and miniskirt, but her face was oddly at variance with her trendy outfit. It was the face of somebody who had given up. Her hair had been permed but was growing out unevenly as if she had once tried to look good but had decided it wasn't worth the effort. Her raspberry–colored lipstick had gotten smeared on her teeth.

"Isn't this the limit?" she said. "Everything that *can* go wrong *has* gone wrong. If one more blipping thing happens—I don't know."

Rice made a half-hearted gesture of farewell to us and the two of them left together. The girl's high heels clicked on the floor and her hips swayed as she minced along beside him.

"Who was *that?"* I asked, after they had gone.

My question had been rhetorical, but Enid had the answer. "That's Sue Ann Taylor. Dennis knows her. She's one of the Founding Freshmen. He says she was married and divorced before she even turned sixteen."

I cast a look after them. "There's something about her that reminds you of those big trucks whose brakes have given out—that out-of-control look."

"I have a feeling it's a bad idea for Rice to run around with her, don't you?"

"I'll bet he can take care of himself."

"I think they knew each other in Miami. I wonder what he sees in her."

I figured I knew very well what he saw in her. She had a car.

The next day I handed in my Western Civ. paper. A wave of relief washed over me, but then Professor Stuart gave us the assignment for the next week's paper. All at once I could see Western Civ. papers stretching endlessly before me. No free weekends, just one Western Civ. paper after another my entire freshman year. Ugh.

After this devastating insight, I went by the mail room and found a letter from home in my box. I ripped the letter open. It was Mom's handwriting.

Dear Deborah Susan,

It was great to hear that you are getting along so well at college. Thanks for letting me know that the care package arrived. Don't worry about my going to the trouble. Nothing is too good for my baby!

Frank Jr. fell out of a tree yesterday and had to have six stitches. No concussion, though, thank goodness.

The hardware store has been bought out by a big chain. It was quite a surprise, but maybe we should have seen it coming. The first thing the new firm did was to change the medical insurance and all our pre-existing conditions are excluded under the new system, which is certainly a pain in the neck. I hope my back does not start acting up again. We will just have to cross our fingers about that. Your father really does not like his new boss but he is being very careful not to let him know it. You know your father can be quite a charmer when he puts his mind to it!

We ran short again before payday, but isn't it wonderful that we all like grits! If I win the Publisher's Clearing House sweepstakes, I am going to take the whole family to Paris and we will order five courses everywhere.

Love,
Mom

I did not like the sound of that change in ownership at the store. When you lived with as small a margin of safety as my family did, change was always an anxious thing. Theoretically, things could get better as easily as they could get worse, but in my actual experience they usually got worse.

I came out of the mail room blinking in the bright sunlight and ran smack into James.

"Whoa," he said, holding onto my arms. "Steady. I didn't do it, honest I didn't."

"What?"

"You're frowning in a very fierce way, in case you haven't noticed."

I stuffed the letter into my jeans pocket. "I was probably squinting against the sun."

He fell into step beside me. "I guess you're seeing a lot more of Dennis these days than I am, huh?"

"He is over at the room a fair amount," I admitted.

"So, I guess I know where to find him if I ever want to see him again."

"Okay, I admit it—he and Enid are inseparable. It turned out you were right about that."

James bared his teeth and drew his finger across his neck in a cutting gesture. "Kiss of death," he said. "Coupledom."

I grinned.

"How are your classes going?" he asked.

I started to tell the truth about my slaving all weekend on the Western Civ. paper but I remembered just in time that Dusty wasn't a grind.

I thought a second. "Fun," I said.

"Fun? Your classes are fun? Are we going to the same school or what?"

"Well, interesting, you know."

"What time are you and the love birds going to dinner tonight?"

"About five-thirty, probably."

"I'll see you there. I have to hear more about this fun time you're having." He lifted his hand in farewell as he veered off toward the auditorium.

I watched as he walked away. I was trying to remember that Dusty probably believed in playing the field as I stood there listening to the rhythm of my heart.

"Boo!" said Ann. "Are you in a trance or something?" She fanned three letters out in one hand and regarded them with satisfaction. "Doesn't it just cheer you up incredibly to get letters from home?"

Not exactly, I thought, but I didn't tell her that.

"Tell me, do you think long distance relationships

61

can last?" Ann asked. Her brow was creased. I noticed then that one of her letters had been written on Georgia Tech stationary.

"I'm not sure."

"I think they can," she said decisively.

I watched her bouncy step as she headed in the direction of the dorm. Nobody I knew seemed more open and honest than Ann. She was so different from me. But after all, even Ann had a secret—she made her own clothes. It was just possible that almost all my friends were concealing something, even if it was only what nerds they had been in high school.

And why not? Who could possibly pass up the chance to start fresh when they went away to school? I had a perfect right to begin all over. The only thing was it was sometimes kind of a strain being Dusty. Sometimes I would have liked to quit being strong and cool and just let myself burst into tears. I sighed heavily as I moved off toward the classroom buildings.

That night, James showed up at our table as promised.

"You know what Dusty gets off on, folks? No, don't hold your breath. It can be revealed but it's more perverted than you could ever guess—calculus and Western Civ. No joke. She admitted it to me. Fun she called it. I think we ought to have the girl tested. There may be significant personality disturbance."

"Class can be sort of interesting," said Enid. "Not calculus maybe, but Western Civ."

I stuck out my tongue at James. He grinned at me, and I immediately felt warm down to my toes.

"You know what Paul's mother gets off on?" Carol put in gloomily.

"I'm afraid to ask," said James.

"Embroidery. She's already started making our wedding gift. It's going to be a cutwork, embroidered tablecloth."

"That will be lovely," said Enid. "My mother has one."

Carol paused meaningfully, "She's doing it in all six primary colors. And we'll probably have to use it every time she comes to dinner."

There was a moment of respectful silence as we all considered what a blow this would be to one of Carol's carefully muted color schemes.

Then she shrugged. "Oh, well, I should look on the bright side. The woman can't live forever."

Enid looked at me and rolled her eyes, but I scarcely noticed. I was looking out the big window, watching the sailboats moored where the creek emptied into the bay. Someone seemed to be taking one out. A sail had been hoisted and was beginning to billow in the breeze.

"Are you interested in sailing, Dusty?" asked James, looking up from cutting his meat.

"I've never been out on a boat, actually." I had the uncomfortable feeling that it came out sounding like a shameful admission.

"I'll take you out. Always looking for new recruits for the sailing club."

"Don't go," advised Carol. "When you go with James you never get to sail. You always end up just handing him drinks and sandwiches. Then he makes you stow the sails afterwards."

"Black lies. Maybe I did get a little carried away

with enthusiasm once or twice, but it was a momentary lapse."

"Don't say you weren't warned," said Carol.

I wondered whether to mention that I couldn't swim. I decided against it. I didn't want to take the chance on James rescinding his invitation.

"I'd like to go sailing," I said quickly.

That fleeting smile lit James's face and I felt strangely happy. I couldn't wait to hand him sandwiches and cold drinks and to "stow the sails," whatever that meant.

When we got back to the dorm, a sheet of paper had been pushed under our door announcing a special dorm meeting. When Carol went by I waved the sheet at her. "What's this about?"

"We've had some complaints about girls ironing in the nude."

"People are ironing in the nude?"

"Come to the meeting," Carol said, "and find out all about it."

At eleven the dorm meeting convened in the downstairs lounge with most of the girls dressed in their pajamas. Enid nudged me. "There's the girl from your hometown," she said. "Do you see her over there?"

I saw her all right. Just being in the same room with Margaret made me feel awkward and brunette. Knowing that she remembered the old me and that she still saw me as Deborah Susan was deeply unnerving. I felt as if she were about to point at me and shout, "You were a twelfth-grade nothing." It didn't help that every time she saw me with my new platinum blond hair a look of surprise and amusement crept over her face.

"Do you know her?" whispered Enid.

"I know her slightly," I whispered back. "But we don't have anything in common."

Debate on the nudity-in-ironing issue was spirited.

"I don't know about you," said the brunette with the plump arms, "but I get hot when I iron. The air-conditioning upstairs is a joke. It's different for all you people downstairs."

"Elaine is making a good point. It *is* hot upstairs. Come up to my room sometime and see," said a girl with dots of Clearasil all over her face.

"Okay, it's hot," said a girl in a cotton nightgown, "particularly if you're one of those who could stand to take off a few pounds. But I still say you ought to pull your curtains closed if you want to dance around naked."

"I think we should try to keep from getting personally offensive," said Elaine coldly.

"I'm not being offensive. I'm just speaking plainly."

Elaine held up a hand. "Marion, if you please—do you mind letting me finish?"

"So finish."

"Thank you. We are not dancing around naked. We're just trying to maintain a neat appearance and when the curtains are pulled the light isn't good enough to iron by."

Margaret spoke in bland deliberate syllables. "There are a number of very nice, loose house dresses that are cool enough for ironing. My mother has some. I could have her send us some samples . . ."

Elaine hooted.

"So what is this?" asked Laurie. "Are we ashamed of our bodies or what? I mean, after all this is the way God made us!"

The girl in the cotton nightgown folded her arms across her chest. "If we must bring up the subject of God . . ." she began portentously.

"Marion has a good point," chimed in another girl. "We can't forget there is a moral side to this question."

I began to perceive that basically two factions were heatedly involved in the debate—the God Squad group, with heavy strength on the ground floor, and the Free Spirits who seemed to be clustered among the upperclassmen on the top floor.

"This is a case of individual freedom," said Elaine grandly. "As John Stuart Mill pointed out, when the state usurps the power that should belong to the individual you have tyranny."

"Are you calling me a communist?" said the girl in the cotton nightgown, her face growing pink.

"All I'm saying is I don't tell *you* how to do your ironing."

A girl in pigtails spoke for the first time. "Well, I just don't want people to burst out laughing when I tell them I live in Grant, that's all. We're talking about the reputation of the dorm."

"I don't believe for a minute you can see inside the rooms unless you get right up to the screens," put in the girl next to Elaine.

"People do get up against the screens. You know how boys are always sitting on that brick railing and leaning against the windows on the ground floor. I got up one morning and was practically nose to nose with this guy who was practicing his guitar outside my window."

Carol glanced at her watch. "I think each side should nominate someone to conduct an objective experiment to see exactly what the visibility is from the outside."

"I volunteer to be the naked person," Laurie said, throwing her arms in the air exuberantly.

"That figures," muttered the girl in the cotton nightgown.

"Okay, Marion Henderson, what exactly do you mean by that!"

One remark led to another, and another, and it was getting on toward midnight when Enid and I finally got back to our room. "What did you think about all that?" I asked her.

"I'm too tired to care," she said, flopping into her bed. "I wish they would all move to some other dorm and give us some peace."

"Well," I said, pulling the sheet up to my chin. "Whatever else you can say about this place, it's not dull."

Chapter Six

I met James at the dock the next day. He was already in one of the sailboats, busying himself with ropes and dirty white canvas. He was wearing tight and disreputable jeans with an old windbreaker. My heart turned over at the sight of him.

He looked up and smiled at me. "Hi, Dusty."

I smiled. It was almost too good to be true. This had to be somebody else's life. Unconsciously, I began looking around for the catch.

"You do have life jackets, don't you?"

"Never go out without them. Sailing club rule. You aren't nervous or anything, are you?"

"It's just that I can't swim."

"Can't swim?" His eyes widened. He quickly added, "No problem. You can practically walk across the bay here anyway. And you'll have your life jacket. Get in."

I didn't like the way the boat wobbled when I stepped in and the orange life jacket he handed me looked grimy. But neither of those things bothered me as much as the way his eyes had widened when I confessed I couldn't swim. It was at moments like this that I felt bitter about my family's not belonging to a country club. I wished I had been ferried to swimming lessons and tennis lessons like all the smooth, cool kids. I wished I had not confessed that I couldn't swim.

I heard a flapping sound and saw that the sail was filling with air.

"A small boat like this, one person can handle," James said.

The boat slipped away from the dock and onto the open water of the bay in perfect silence almost before I realized we were underway. I was amazed at its lightness and quickness.

"Theoretically, a sailboat has the right of way," James said, "but there are so many congenital idiots out on the water, you have to keep your eyes out for them."

A motorboat blared through the shining water beyond us and a moment later we rocked in its wake.

"I don't know why anybody would want to go around in one of those things when they could go like this," I said.

"This is the way to go, all right," said James. "You notice how you never see advertisements for sailboats? That's because sailing is a natural human instinct."

The bay was sequined with dimples of light and I felt a rush of exhilaration. This was the sort of thing I had dreamed of, skating along the water with the wind.

Around us the water lay broad and blue as peace. And the boat, the perfect creature of wind and water, cut through it. It was the closest thing to flying I would ever feel.

"Want to hand me a sandwich?" he said.

I turned to grope in the picnic bag, trying not to look amused.

"Okay, I know what you're thinking, but it's not true. That time I took Carol out I hadn't been sailing for weeks. I had the flu or something. It was like getting out of prison. I wasn't in my right mind the first day I got out on the water. Besides, she doesn't like to sail anyway. She was just giving me a hard time."

I handed him the sandwich and then popped open a cold drink for myself. A gull wheeled overhead, squawking.

I looked up at the sail. "Does the wind ever give out?" I asked. "I mean, could a person just get stuck out here on the bay?"

"Kind of a worrier, aren't you?"

"No, not at all," I said quickly. "I was just curious. I wouldn't care if we get stuck out here."

He grinned. "Neither would I."

The wind felt cool on my hot cheeks. I felt as if we had crossed the boundary between friendliness and flirtation and I wasn't sure what came next.

"We aren't likely to get stuck, though," he said. "If there's any wind out here at all the sails will find it, and you can always tack. Maybe once in a while, somebody will be becalmed out here. Blake never has exactly straightened out whether that merits an excused absence from class or not." He grinned at me.

James went on talking about sailing. I couldn't follow half of it, but I didn't mind. I enjoyed seeing the pleasure on his face.

"Did you decide to go to Blake because of the sailing?" I asked after a while.

He hesitated. "Well, no."

A silence fell between us.

I was careful not to ask a probing question. Everybody was entitled to secrets. I didn't want people asking *me* nosy questions.

"I guess I spend more time out here than I should," he said finally. "I'm kind of a wharf rat. Brought up around boats. When I get fed up with stuff I like to just take a boat out and . . ." His voice trailed off.

"Think?"

He grinned. "No. *Not* think."

"I can understand that." I leaned over the edge of the boat and trailed my fingers in the water. The sun was hot on my back as I watched the water splaying out from my fingers in a tiny wake. "Do you ever get the feeling," I said, "that you aren't exactly sure who you are?"

I turned to watch him as he rearranged the sails. It seemed to involve a lot of ropes.

"Nah, I don't think so," he said finally. "Do you?"

"All the time."

"That's funny," he said, "because offhand, I can't think of anybody that hits me as more definite personality."

"I don't feel very definite."

"Sure you are. The minute I met you I had this feeling about it. This one's going to get what she wants, I said to myself."

"I sound charming," I said gloomily.

He smiled at me. "Well, I thought so." He looked toward shore. "We'd better be getting back."

The boat wheeled around and headed back. I

rested my chin on my hand and gazed at the brick college buildings on the distant shore. Had James really said I was charming? It had sounded like it. I wished I had the whole thing on tape so I could run it by me again. "I wish we didn't have to get back," I said. "I wish we could just sail and sail and keep going around the world."

"That's a pretty far piece, but I'm game."

"In a beautiful pea green boat. We'd take some honey and plenty of money . . ."

"Wrapped up in a five-pound note," he finished. "But I don't think the owl and the pussycat had to make it to classes. Lucky ducks."

When we got back to the dock, he leapt off the boat and tied it up, then he reached out to me. I grabbed his hand. The boat moved under my feet and knocked against the dock as I made the jump out. "Phew," I said. I was relieved that my feet had made it to solid ground.

"Now, you be sure and tell Carol that I let you sail all you wanted to."

"Oh, absolutely."

"And you've got to learn to swim, Dusty. You can't sail around the world until you do. Or even join the sailing club, for that matter."

"Maybe I'll just have to limit myself to handing you drinks and sandwiches."

He grinned. "Well, that would be all right, too, I guess."

My skin felt tight and prickly from being in the sun so long. Tomorrow my face would be lobster pink, but it had been worth it. I was feeling pleased with life as I walked back to the dorm.

When I got back, I ran into Meg and Elaine in the hall near my room.

"Two of them in our own dorm," Elaine moaned. "We won't be able to call our soul our own. It's like cohabiting with the KGB."

"Two of what?" I asked.

Meg pushed her hair out of her face so she could see me and smiled at me. "Two honor court justices. Margaret and Marion both got elected."

"How nice," I said.

I think it was then I realized that people in my very own dorm were doing things that were in violation of the honor code. I hadn't had the faintest suspicion of it till then. Nobody had invited me to do anything in violation of the honor code. I was a little hurt. True, it might be the kind of thing I didn't want to get involved with—drugs, wild parties, orgies, a theft ring, something like that. But it would have been nice to be asked. After all, Meg had obviously been included and she wasn't exactly Miss Charm.

That may have been why I didn't turn down the invitation that came the following weekend.

"Elaine wants to know if we want to go drinking," Enid said Saturday night. "They're going off campus so it will be perfectly safe. I think I'm going to go. With Dennis gone every weekend, I get so tired of sitting around the dorm."

"But where would you get the liquor?"

"Rice can get me a bottle. He keeps a full bar in his room. And for that matter, Elaine will probably take a list by the liquor store this afternoon and get what everybody wants."

I realized that was the sort of adventure Dusty

would definitely say yes to, so I ignored the cowardly voice of Deborah Susan inside of me. "Maybe we could split a bottle," I said.

"What do you drink?"

Actually, what I drank was orangeade, but I did not want to say that. I had already admitted I did not swim and then regretted it. I wasn't about to admit I didn't drink. "Whatever you want would be okay," I said.

"What I like is that soda pop wine. You know the stuff you see in the grocery store with oranges and stuff on the label? But I'm afraid if we get that they might laugh at us. What do you say we go with scotch? Nobody laughs at that and you can drink it plain without messing with ice and soda and all that. We're going to be out in the woods and I doubt if Elaine is providing swizzle sticks."

That seemed to make sense. I certainly didn't want people to laugh at me.

About an hour after dark, we drove off campus in Elaine's Volkswagen. It was crammed so incredibly full with people that somebody's knee stayed jammed against my eye half of the way. A nauseatingly warm breath of peppermint fell on my face. One of my fellow passengers was a chewer of breath mints.

"We'll go to this secret place I know about," said Elaine.

I felt the car careen out on the main highway and I heard all the bottles go clink. Somebody's elbow jammed into my ribs. I squirmed and managed to see out the window that we were turning again and were passing by Lou's Diner.

"How far is it?" asked Enid.

"Not far. That's the neat thing about it," said Elaine.

"Oomph," said Enid.

I presumed somebody's knee had ended up in her stomach. Half of the people in the car were people I didn't know, though their faces looked vaguely familiar. One in particular, a tall silent blond boy called Jeff should have been left out, in my opinion, for reasons of space limitations. He not only had sharp elbows and knees but more of them than I would have believed humanly possible.

"We're almost there," said Elaine.

The car began to bump wildly so I deduced we had turned onto a dirt road. At last we came to a stop.

"Here we are," said Elaine.

We all scrambled awkwardly out of the car.

"Isn't this neat?" said Elaine. "Nobody else knows about it."

The branches showed up inky black against the very faint gray glow of the night sky and I could hear the whispering of wind in the high trees. In the other direction I saw a glow of light I realized must be from the sign out in front of Lou's. I was glad I had discerned that faint landmark because except for that, the place was like an exercise in sensory deprivation—everything was black and silent.

"Did anybody bring a blanket?"

"I've got blankets."

"There aren't any cows out here are there? I would hate to meet up with a cow."

"Of course not, idiot. You don't see any fences do you?"

"I don't see anything. Geez, it's dark."

"Well, I can't leave the car lights on. The police are always patrolling around the college."

Great. Just what I needed to hear to put my mind at ease.

We gathered up the bottles, blankets, and cups and walked out of sight of the car while Elaine waxed rhapsodic about what a perfect spot she had found. Then we spread out the blankets and started drinking. My first taste of scotch was a shock. I had never tasted anything so vile. I decided that scotch was to taste as gasoline was to smell. The stuff actually burned my throat.

"This is nice," someone said.

I looked around in astonishment but it was so dark I couldn't make out the face of the idiot who said it.

After that, nobody said much. There were long silences when the only noise heard was the wind in the trees and the clinking of bottles. I watched the branches moving against the evening sky, conscious that my face was starting to feel funny and warm.

"I'm afraid I may be taking more than my share," Enid said.

"Help yourself." I handed her the bottle. I felt strange. I wasn't sure if it was the scotch or the sensory deprivation but I decided I had probably had enough. I poured the rest of what was in my plastic glass out on the ground, although I was pretty sure it would kill the grass.

"Geez!" someone whispered suddenly. "It's the cops!"

"Where?"

"See that flashing blue light?"

I was so startled that my contact lenses slipped

and everything went blurry. I was aware of faint sounds of scuffling as everyone scrambled up and rushed off. Unfortunately, I didn't dare move.

I forced myself to stay calm. After all, I was not far from the college so it didn't matter if they left without me. And if I stayed still I didn't see how the police could see me even if they drove right up to the field. My immediate problem was only how to get my lenses back on my eyes when they were lodged uncomfortably somewhere up under my lids. I had to be careful not to flip them out accidentally onto the ground in the dark field because if I did, I would never be able to find them again and I couldn't afford to buy another pair. It had taken me half of one summer to earn the money for these. I gingerly lay down on my back. Then I stared up at the sky and started pushing against my eyelids, trying to get my lenses back in place. I kept imagining I heard sinister sounds in the underbrush but at that point I had other worries. My contact lenses seemed to be held against my eyeball by unbelievably strong suction.

When at last, the lenses popped back into place, the distant trees came back into focus and I heaved a sigh of relief. I could see. I blinked carefully. It seemed the lenses were on pretty well now. I could make out the lights of Lou's sign on the highway and the distant lights of the passing cars on the highway. I just needed to find my way to the dirt road to find my way home. I could make out that there were trees in one direction and in the other there seemed to be a clearing. I walked toward the clearing. A minute later, I could see the light reflecting faintly off the light dirt of the road. To my surprise, I saw Elaine's Volkswagen.

Enid said softly, "Dusty?"

"Is that you, Dusty?" said Elaine. "Golly, what a relief."

"My contact lenses slipped. I thought you all had gone on."

"You didn't think we were going to leave you, did you?" said Elaine. "We couldn't figure out what happened. It was like you dropped down a black hole. I didn't even have a flashlight to go look for you with."

"What happened to the cops?"

"I guess they drove on by. They didn't come down the dirt road."

"What a waste of good liquor," complained Jeff. "I'm cold sober already."

Elaine threw the car door open for me.

"Ouch," said someone. "Jeff, your elbow is in my eye."

"You go on," I said. "I'll walk back."

"We can't let you walk back alone," said Enid.

"Are you drunk?" asked Elaine.

"I'm fine," I said. "I just want some fresh air."

"It's probably two miles to the dorm," warned Elaine. "Are you sure you're okay?"

"I'm absolutely fine."

"I wish you would get in, Dusty," said Enid.

"Well, we can't make her, guys," said Elaine. "Okay, if that's what you want to do. But if you're not back at the dorm by midnight I'm reporting you to the police as a missing person."

She started up the motor and drove off. I watched the taillights of the Volkswagen bump down the dirt road and disappear, then I started out walking in the same direction. I felt lucky not to have Jeff's elbow in my eye.

It was only a short walk to Lou's, a diner the shape and size of a railway car. I smelled hamburger cooking and decided to treat myself to a sandwich.

I ran my hand over my hair, checking for twigs and leaves that might have caught in it. Sure enough, a small brown leaf fluttered down to my shoes. I gave my hair a final pat then pushed the diner's door open.

Inside was a faint haze of smoke from the grill and the pervasive smell of cooking meat. At the end of the counter stood a barrel of kosher pickles.

"Dusty!"

Startled, I looked up and saw James sitting at a back booth. He looked as dark as a gypsy in the gloom and the smoke haze. I went over to him. He was sitting next to the pickle barrel.

"How's your sunburn?"

"Better," I said. "Enid's been swabbing me down with Solarcaine."

"Sit down," he said. "I've never seen you over here before. What brings you out this way?"

"Hunger," I said, sliding into the booth. I pulled a wrinkled five-dollar bill from my pocket. I was already regretting the money I had spent on the half bottle of scotch.

"I can recommend the hot pastrami," said James.

After a glance at the laminated plastic menu I decided the foot-long hot dog was more in my price range.

"Let me treat you," said James.

I darted a quick look up at him, wondering if he somehow guessed how straitened my finances were.

"It doesn't commit you to anything," he said hastily. "I just got my allowance and I'm all excited to see a friendly face."

"Okay. That would be nice. Maybe I will have a hot pastrami."

"You won't regret it."

I stretched my legs out under the table. I was feeling lucky. Escaping a prowling police car can make you feel that way, I discovered. And coming upon James all of a sudden made it even better.

James put in the order for the pastrami and requested extra hot mustard and a side order of fries.

"The fries are for me," he said. "But you can have some." He reached over and plucked a brown leaf from my hair.

"Do you see any more?" I asked anxiously. I ran my fingers over my hair again and disentangled a twig.

"I think we got it all. What did you say brought you out in this direction?" His eyes were noncommittal.

"You aren't on the honor court, by any chance, are you?"

He shook his head.

"Well, actually, I was going drinking."

"And that's how you got twigs in your hair?" He hesitated. "Uh, how much drinking did you do exactly?"

I realized he was imagining I had passed out cold and I hastened to explain. "The twigs were because somebody thought they saw the police and then my contact lenses slipped so I had to lie back to try to fix them, and—oh, it's a long story."

"Here comes our food."

I was amazingly hungry. I hated to think what Ann would have said about a hot pastrami sandwich but I enjoyed every greasy calorie.

"I've never been much for going drinking," said James. "Whenever I used to do it I always got covered with chinch bugs and spent the whole night itching all over."

Suddenly, I itched all over. I pushed up my sleeve and scratched.

"Sorry about that," said James. "Power of suggestion, I guess."

"How can you tell if you've got chinch bug bites?"

He examined my legs. "Here," he said, extending a finger. "See these little red spots? Those are chinch bug bites."

I scratched. "How long do they itch?"

"A day or two. They say you can kill them by painting colorless fingernail polish on the spots. Do you want that last french fry?"

"Yes." I stuffed it in my mouth.

"Are you ready to walk home, now?"

Outside, a haze of gnats, attracted by the light, were flying around the big sign that said "Lou's." In front of us, cars whizzed by on the highway at a frightening speed. James put his hand at the small of my back and we hurried across to the safety island.

"I'm not cut out for this kind of thing," I said with a shudder when we were safely on the other side of the road. "I should have been born back in the days when people had addresses like Rose Cottage, Windemere . . . the days of the horse and buggy."

"Well, you seem sober enough, anyway. I think you could dodge a car, if you had to," said James.

"I'm not much of a drinker," I said. As soon as I said that, I knew it was true.

"I'm no drinker either," he said. "That's one of the things Dennis and I have in common. In an otherwise hard-drinking school, we are islands of sobriety."

"I didn't realize Blake was a hard-drinking school."

"Well, maybe it's not if you compare it to fraternity life at big universities. But it's surprising how much time people spend either talking about going drinking, going drinking or figuring out how to go drinking."

I looked at him, but we were out of the reach of the highway lights now and I couldn't see him very well.

"Do you by any chance," I suggested hesitantly, "have some personal reason for not liking drinking?"

"Nope. It just doesn't appeal to me. Sometimes I hear guys coming in at night throwing up all over the place, crashing around in their rooms and I think, 'This is fun?' It's a matter of taste. For Dennis it's different. He doesn't say much, but I know it makes him crazy. It sticks out all over him when some dumb bozo stumbles in dead drunk. He'll just turn his back and walk away, but it does something to him. I guess you know about his sister and all?"

I nodded.

"He told me once that every drunk person he ever sees reminds him of Roger. It's like a visceral reaction. This anger comes sweeping over him and he just can't handle it."

"I can understand that."

"Oh, sure. Me, too. The thing is, you can't get away from your experience. Everybody's haunted by his past. No, maybe that's not the best way to say it. Everybody is shaped by his past. A person's past makes him who he is."

"You sound like you're saying there's no such thing as free will."

"I guess I'm not a major believer in free will."

"You're a Presbyterian, I'll bet. Predestination."

"It's not that," he protested. "Just look around you. Half the people you see are basically predictable. It's like they're programmed. If you know the basic package of genes the person inherited, and you know their past, I think you can tell what they're going to be like."

"Bosh!"

"What did you say?"

"Bosh! I don't believe it."

"You crack me up, the things you say. Bosh, indeed!"

"I mean people aren't predictable. If they were you could hand out grades at the beginning of the semester."

"You probably could if biology were more perfectly understood. If you really knew right down to the last gene what somebody had inherited and what had happened to him since, you could predict his grades."

I scratched my arm. "Pure theory. That's all the evidence you've got."

"The evidence is incomplete maybe, but it points in that direction."

"I don't believe it. People don't inherit who they are. They *decide* who they are."

I had the feeling I was speaking a bit too loudly. I guess this question of identity was really bothering me. What was an identity? Could anyone trade an old one in for a new one? Could I?

"Watch it," he said, grabbing hold of my arm. "The ground's pretty uneven here."

I could see the lights of the dorms ahead and to the west the headlights of cars moving across the Skyway Bridge.

Then James pulled me closer to him and kissed me. He smelled faintly of pickles and pastrami, and I could feel his warmth through his thin shirt. A feeling of peace stole over me as we clung to each other. It seemed stupid that we had just been standing around arguing about predestination.

In the distance, the lights of cars on the Skyway Bridge moved quietly on, a never-ending necklace of luminescence.

Chapter Seven

A little later, Enid and I sat on our beds painting colorless fingernail polish on our chinch bites.

"I ran into James over at Lou's Diner," I said with studied casualness. "He bought me a hot pastrami."

Enid arched her tiny foot and painted dabs of fingernail polish on the instep. "You're seeing a lot of him lately, aren't you?"

"Oh, well—I guess."

She grinned. "I told you he was interested in you. I already asked Dennis about him and he told me James isn't seeing anybody else."

The very idea of James going out with someone else almost knocked the breath out of me. I hadn't even thought about the possibility.

"I guess Dennis would know if he were seeing someone," I said finally.

"Oh, yeah. They're very tight." Enid extended one leg and considered her handiwork. "You know, I don't think I like going out drinking the way we did tonight."

"Me either." Pleased we had come to the same conclusion, I blew on the fingernail polish to make it dry faster.

"It's uncivilized." Enid got down on her knees and groped under the bed for the bottle of scotch. She held it up to the light. "We've still got a lot of it left. I think it makes more sense to have a drink here in our room instead of going out in the woods and getting chewed up by bugs, don't you?"

I looked up quickly. "You'd better lock the door if you're going to do that," I said.

Enid thrust the bottle back under the bed. "The only thing is I'm not that crazy about scotch. Do you want to go halves on a bottle of rum? I'm sure Rice could get it for us. Then we could mix it with cola from the soft drink machine, and have Cuba Libres. Cuba Libres are almost like drinking plain Coke."

Then why not drink a plain Coke? I found myself thinking. Fewer calories, it's not against the rules, and it tastes better. I didn't say that, however. I had a horror that if I opened my mouth, I might end up sounding like Margaret Wentworth.

"Hmm," she said. "I wonder what scotch and cola would taste like?"

She brought back a cola from the drink machine and poured some scotch into the paper cup. After stirring it with the sharpened end of a pencil, she took a sip. "Not bad," she said. "Tastes a little funny, though. Want a taste?"

"No, thank you." Even though it was quite late, there was always the remote chance Margaret might show up at the door to give me another pitch for her prayer group, and the very thought of it gave me the jitters. "I'm not really much of a drinker," I added.

"If we had a refrigerator," Enid said, "we could

do brandy Alexanders, frozen daiquiris, the works. Would you be interested in going halves on a small refrigerator?"

"No." I was beginning to have a bad feeling about this drinking. I mean, when you can't tell the difference between your roommate's conversation and a bar list, it's bound to give you the creeps. But I couldn't live Enid's life for her.

Monday morning I got my first Western Civ. paper back from Dr. Stuart. I got an A. I leafed through the pages looking for comments. "Clear, insightful, well-reasoned. I expected good work from you, Dusty, and I have not been disappointed."

When I read that, I had the funny sensation that the praise was for someone else—for Dusty. It was as if I were standing off at a distance watching Dusty get my first A. This business of changing my identity had turned out to be uncomfortable in a few ways I hadn't anticipated.

Next I went by the post office and found a letter from Mom waiting for me.

Dear Deborah Susan,

My, have we been having drama here! Do you remember how I told you Frank Jr. fell out of that tree? He was having some back pain, so the doctor thought we had better have him tested to make sure his kidneys were not bruised. It is a very simple test they do at the hospital where they inject red dye and then take a picture of the kidneys. Your father and I were waiting outside the room where they were doing the test and imagine our surprise when a code alert came over the intercom and hordes of men in white coats and tennis shoes came running. Wouldn't you know that Frank Jr. turned out to be allergic to the red dye and that his heart had stopped! Of course, as I told your father, it couldn't have happened in a better place. He was already right there in the hospital and they got his heart beating again right away. They did keep him in overnight for observation. Actually, I suppose his allergy to the red dye is not too surprising. We have always been a *most* allergic family, if I do say so myself. Frank Jr. was mad that he was unconscious through the whole thing. He said it was just like an episode on *General Hospital* and he missed it!

As for the other news, your father absolutely hates his work, but as I tell him you just have to put up with your boss's funny ways, no matter what you think of him.

I'm afraid my back is acting up again.

Love,
Mom

As I edged out of the mail room my books slipped out of my hands. I scooped the books and the letter up off the gritty floor and staggered outside into the sunshine.

What I hated most about letters from home was that when they came I could feel dribbles of Deborah Susan beginning to leak through the cracks in Dusty.

Dusty was all cool confidence. She did not get rattled and drop things. But a letter like this one cracked my Dusty facade to smithereens. It stripped away my confidence. It worried me sick.

I knew Mom did not mean to upset me and chip away at my fragile sense of security. But every letter from home reminded me that I wasn't who I pretended to be. Even the handwriting on the envelope, weirdly reminiscent of my own handwriting, made me feel as if I were linked to bad luck.

I could feel the news from home burning in my chest and my head. I don't need it, I thought desperately, as I squinted into the sunlight, I just don't *need* it.

I went into the campus book shop and bought a funny get well card for Frank Jr. From what Mom said, it sounded as if he were okay now, but a sense of dread still clung to me, the way smoke clings to the clothes of people who have escaped a burning building.

It will always be like this, I thought suddenly. News from my family will always knock me off my feet. I can change my name, I can move away, but when it comes to caring about what happens to them, there is no cure for that.

When I got back to the dorm, Enid said, "Let me show you what I've got."

My mind was so full of Frank Jr.'s close call, I scarcely heard her, but when she opened the two typewriter cases under her bed, suddenly she had my full attention.

"I thought you were just going to get a bottle of rum!" I gasped. "This looks like a liquor store!"

"Rice thought I might as well get an assortment of things until my taste develops and I decide what I really like."

"You don't think you sort of went overboard?"

"Well, this way we can have a civilized drink in here every night before dinner."

"I don't know, Enid. If Dennis ever smelled it on your breath it might be *phht* with you two. He just cannot handle people drinking."

"I hear what you're saying. You're right. I don't want to upset him. A drink before bedtime would be better, anyway. I want to keep my head clear for studying." She shut both typewriter cases and pushed them back under the bed. She smiled at me. "Did you hear yourself saying *phht* just then? You're starting to talk like James."

I hugged my knees. "I guess I don't have a very secure sense of identity," I muttered.

"I don't know why you're blushing. You like him, and it's obvious he likes you."

It sounded so simple when she put it that way. But the truth was more complicated. Dusty was the kind of girl who could take 'em or leave 'em. She was the epitome of cool. That was a tricky facade for me to maintain under the best circumstances and well nigh impossible when things were going wrong at home and when on top of that I seemed to be falling in love. I was always off balance.

Luckily, there were distractions. I had other things to do than sit around and worry about myself. For example, the following week another dorm meeting was called. Marion Henderson presented a snapshot taken with telephoto lens which, she said, clearly showed Elaine ironing in the nude.

We all crowded around to look at it. It was pretty good of the geranium at the edge of the window sill, but a lot of reflection was bouncing off the big plate-glass window and all I could make out behind it was a pale shape which, I suppose, could have been Elaine. But it also could have been anything. It reminded me of those pictures you're always seeing of flying saucers.

"You've got it all wrong, Marion," said Elaine. "That's not me. That's my old white sweatshirt hanging on an open closet door."

"Maybe the lighting was not exactly ideal," Marion retorted. "I don't pretend to be a professional photographer, but believe me, it was a lot clearer when seen with the naked eye."

"Maybe you ought to talk to somebody about this fixation you have about nakedness," said Elaine kindly.

"Now, listen here," sputtered Marion, "I'm prepared to take this matter to the administration. Or higher! To the board of trustees even!"

Elaine considered her fingernails. "Be cool, Marion. We all want to live in peace with our neighbors, I'm sure. I know I speak for everyone on the top floor when I say that."

"Sure," chimed in Laurie.

"Does this mean you're going to wear clothes when you iron?" asked Marion suspiciously.

"Absolutely."

The group of girls near Elaine nodded in unison.

"I think that's just wonderful," Margaret said. Her pink cheeks were flushed with genuine pleasure. "This is a real case of democracy in action. I think it's just great the way we've worked all this out, and I also want to say how much I'm sure we all appreciate the spirit of cooperation we see here."

The meeting broke up and we trudged back toward our rooms.

"Are you really going to start wearing clothes when you iron?" I asked Elaine and Laurie when we got upstairs.

"Not on your life," said Elaine.

"Marion doesn't seem to realize it, but it's a free country," said Laurie.

"So what do you think they're going to do? Post a sentinel with binoculars outside our windows for the next six months?" added Elaine. "What they don't know won't hurt them."

"Je-rusalem," I said to Enid when we got back to the room. "What next? Marion is going to be apoplectic if she finds out. This could get embarrassing. Can't you see it? Marion and her friends picketing in front of the dorm. Editorials in the school newspaper. Think about it. Do we really want to be known as the girls from the nudist dorm?"

Enid stretched and yawned. "Don't worry, Dusty. I expect it's all going to die down pretty soon."

"What makes you think that?"

She crawled in her bed. "We're into October. Pretty soon a cold front has got to be moving in."

I realized she was probably right. Once Elaine and her friends started getting goose bumps all over, they would be bound to reach for their clothes. But then Elaine's nudist tendencies were, after all, only a small part of what was bothering me.

I lay awake in bed for quite awhile, thinking about my family. I kept turning over, twisting up my sheets in a futile attempt to get comfortable. Finally, I kicked the sheets untucked. "Great," I breathed. "Just super." I got out of bed and awkwardly tucked them back in. I got back in bed and stared at the ceiling at the faint dots of light projected through the blinds from some light outside. I wondered why when I got into bed at night I always felt like Deborah Susan instead of Dusty.

The following weekend, Dennis took Enid home with him to meet his parents. My spirits were not exactly soaring to begin with, and after Enid left, I felt even lower. Saturday night, I asked Ann if she'd like to go over to the union with me. She snapped at the invitation so fast I realized she was feeling lonely, too.

"I don't realize how much I count on Enid," I said as we walked over to the union, "until she goes away like this."

When we got up to the snack bar, I said, "The usual," and pushed my dime across the counter. I had gotten past the need for subterfuge. I had come to realize that using cafeteria tea bags to save money was pretty mild as college eccentricities went.

Ann got coffee and a doughnut and we found a booth.

She bit into her doughnut, and raspberry jelly oozed over the sides of it. "I guess you and Enid have gotten really close, huh? It's great the way you two get on."

"So, how do you and Meg get on?" I asked. "Okay?"

"Oh, fine."

"That's good."

"But I've never known anybody who was quite so interested in boys," she burst out. She immediately subsided into guilty silence.

I swished my tea bag back and forth in my cup. "A lot of people are interested in boys," I said. As a matter of fact, I was awfully interested in one myself. "I guess it's natural," I added.

"Oh, sure," she said, looking gloomy.

I began to perceive that Ann had been brought up in the school of "if you can't say anything nice, don't say anything at all," a precept which can put a real damper on conversation when you're talking about somebody like Meg.

"Two completely different personalities are bound to have trouble adjusting to living together," I offered.

"Oh, Dusty, I know she doesn't mean any harm, but sometimes she drives me crazy. I took her to church with me and she got something going with the choir director. Last week, she went to this soda shop near one of the high schools and picked up a high school junior."

"Whatever happened to Brandon?"

"Not kinky enough. There was no reason in the world she shouldn't go out with Brandon, so she lost interest right away. Particularly when she found out it wasn't that serious between him and Laurie. If you ask me, it's not so much that she likes boys as that she wants to be somebody's guilty secret. Is that sick or what?"

"It is a strange taste."

"Goodness, I feel awful talking about her like this. After all, Meg is neat and clean and she doesn't smoke or stay up real late. I have a lot to be thankful for." She brooded, staring into her coffee. "If she would just quit bringing me coconut cake and acting like her feelings are hurt if I don't eat it."

"Ladies?"

I looked up quickly at the sound of James's voice. He slid in the booth beside me. I smiled at him.

"Do you have roommate problems, James?" Ann asked.

"I've got a single. You've got roommate problems?"

"Ann's roommate keeps bringing her coconut cake."

"She knows I can't resist it and when I tell her I'm trying to cut back on calories she looks all hurt and says, 'But I know it's your favorite.' "

"Tell you what. You could wrap it up carefully in tin foil and bring it right over to my dorm and I'll take care of it for you."

"It is a hostile thing for her to do, isn't it, Dusty? I'm not just imagining it?"

"Of course, you're not imagining it." Now that James had taken my hand in his, I noticed it was hard for me to get the proper note of indignation in my voice.

"I just can't stand these games people play," Ann said desperately.

James walked with us back to the dorm. The moon was full and yellow overhead and the sidewalk from the union was white in the moonlight.

"Do you want to come on in?" I asked him. "I could fix us all some popcorn."

"Sure."

We all went up to my room and James sat on my bed. I didn't look at him. I was busy with oil and popcorn, but I was very conscious of his presence. It was as if I had a porthole in my skull.

"So this is your room," he said. "What a fantastic collection of swizzle sticks!"

"You are not the first to admire it," I said.

I couldn't tell him so, but the swizzle stick collection was Enid's. She and Rice had gotten in the habit of taking a pair of phony I.D.'s to the Mai Tai Bar and Grill. There they sampled a variety of exotic cocktails while watching the lighted city from the revolving bar. Enid was developing her taste.

James pulled one of the swizzle sticks out of the cup on the bookcase and looked at me questioningly. "The Mai Tai Bar and Grill?"

"A troll I know frequents the place," I said. "Do you like butter on your popcorn?"

"None for me, thanks," said Ann. "I'm sort of trying to cut back."

"You don't need to cut back," said James.

"Go ahead and flatter me," Ann said. "Flattery is the one thing I can eat up without getting fat."

"Why are girls so obsessed with fat?" he asked.

Meg appeared at the door. "Oh, there you are, Annie," she said softly, pushing her hair out of her face with both hands. "Where did you hide the popcorn popper? I can't find it anywhere."

"It's where it always is," said Ann. "In the cubbyhole behind my bed."

"I looked there and I didn't see it." Meg smiled that funny triangular smile that did not reach her eyes. I realized I would go nuts if I had to look at that smile all day. I was amazed Ann was holding up as well as she was.

"It's got to be there. Oh, well, I'll go help you look." Ann got up reluctantly.

After they had gone, James and I sat for a minute

listening to the popcorn popping. He was fiddling with the swizzle sticks. "So that was Ann's famous roommate," he said.

"Notorious is more like it."

"I don't know why Ann can't just tell her what she can do with that coconut cake. What's the big deal?"

"The problem is that Meg is pretending to be nice. If she would just come right out and tell Ann she was trying to fatten her up, Ann would know how to deal with her."

"I doubt it."

"Well, you may be right. I guess that would have its own complications."

"So tell me about this troll that frequents the Mai Tai Bar and Grill."

"Do you know Rice MacEnroe?"

"Freshman? Dark guy with a voice like a foghorn? I know who he is. Runs around with Sue Ellen Taylor."

"She's not much to look at, is she?" I said. I wrinkled my brow in puzzlement. "And she seems just a little bit unglued, too. I wonder if he hangs around with her just so he can use her car."

"He sounds like a terrific fellow. Maybe the real question is why does she hang around with him?"

Actually, this was a question that puzzled me a good deal. How could anybody like Rice? He was so phony, so self-centered. And yet, Enid seemed happy enough to pal around with him. All those drinks at the Mai Tai. All those swizzle sticks. "I think it may be that they're just drinking buddies," I said doubtfully. "He seems to be a very serious drinker. Do you think that kind of thing could be a bond between people?"

"I guess. But I don't think Sue Ellen is a heavy drinker. She's got her faults but that's not among them."

"Of course, maybe she finds him attractive," I said. "Lots of people go for that type. You know, the low voice, the sophisticated air."

James dropped the popcorn bowl and swore. "Look at that," he said remorsefully. "Butter all over your carpet."

We got down on our hands and knees and scrubbed at the carpet with handfuls of Kleenex. Even though we were just cleaning up popcorn, when I got close to him I found myself getting a little breathless.

"I think we've got it all up. It doesn't even show," I said.

He dropped the last few kernels of popcorn, carpet fibers clinging to them, into the wastebasket.

"So are you going out with Rice MacEnroe, or what?" he asked.

"What are you talking about?" I looked at him in astonishment.

"But I thought you were saying ... What about the Mai Tai Bar and Grill?"

"Going out with him? I loathe him!"

His face relaxed into a slow smile.

I couldn't believe that James had really been worried for a minute that I was mixed up with Rice MacEnroe. The whole idea was ridiculous.

But then I remembered how my blood had run cold when Enid had brought up the possibility that there might be other women in James's life. Maybe that kind of fear had to be there when you started to realize how important someone was to you.

"So we're still on for *The Seventh Seal* tomorrow night?"

"Sure."

We smiled at each other happily. I liked him. He liked me. Suddenly, it all seemed very simple.

Chapter Eight

"Dennis's parents are wonderful," Enid said as she unpacked her clothes. "I was nervous at first, wondering whether they would like me or not, but in no time I felt right at home. They're genuine, really good people. When I think of all they've gone through, it's so unfair."

"Rice called while you were gone."

She shook out a shirt and hung it up. "Well, he can call back if it's anything important."

I heard James's knock at the door and moved over to open it. "Ready?" He glanced at Enid. "You going to *The Seventh Seal?*"

"Is that where you guys are off to? Gosh, we're supposed to see it for Western Civ., aren't we? I think I'll catch the Monday afternoon showing instead. I'm pretty tired right now."

I was grateful for Enid's unfailing tact. I most emphatically did not want her along and I think she saw that.

In the moonlight, I could see people streaming toward the auditorium from the dorms. James held my hand as we walked. I glanced at his face. "Is everything all right?"

He smiled down at me. "Sure, everything's fine."

"You look so serious."

He squeezed my hand. "It's all these witnesses," he said. "It's making me queasy. This is where I usually head for the hills."

"Let me get this straight. Are you trying to tell me that holding hands with me in public compromises your reputation?"

"I wouldn't put it that way."

"So, put it in your own words. I'm very interested." I took my hand away from him and put it in my pocket.

"Oh, come on, Dusty. Don't get mad at me."

"I'm not mad at you."

"Liar. It's just that I'm having this funny feeling. I think I'm falling into coupledom."

Well, that was one way to put it.

"Look," I said. "Are you doing anything you don't want to do? Because nobody's got a gun to your back."

"You're taking this all wrong. It's just that it's weird to be on the other side of it all of a sudden. You know, the guys back at the dorm are probably saying, 'Well, I guess we won't be seeing old James around anymore.' Do you see what I mean? They're feeling sorry for me, and heck, now I'm feeling sorry for them."

"Seriously?"

"Yes, seriously. You think I'd rather be sitting around in my undershirt shooting the bull with the guys instead of being here with you? I wouldn't." He put his arm around me and kissed me. I caught a faint whiff of whatever he had put on his hair and felt his sandpaper cheek on mine. "I like you, too," I said.

"So you aren't mad at me anymore?"

"I never was mad at you."

"Liar," he said again. He put an arm around me and we went over to the auditorium.

The next day I had a hard time remembering the fine points of the plot of *The Seventh Seal*. It is very possible that I was not giving it my undivided attention.

It had started getting chilly at night, so when I went to the library the next evening I was careful to take a jacket. When I got back to the dorm later on, I was surprised that our room was dark. I had expected Enid to be there. A little puzzled, I switched the light on.

"Happy birthday!" Enid screeched.

I jumped a mile and was instantly hit with a shower of confetti and paper streamers. The room was full of people.

"G-goodness," I stuttered.

"Were you surprised?" asked Ann.

"Utterly." I plucked a curly paper streamer off of my ear.

Dennis lit the candles on the cake.

"Happy birthday to you," they all sang. "Happy birthday, dear Dusty, happy birthday to you."

"If you blow them all out, you get your wish," said James.

I got up close to the cake and blew out all eighteen candles in a single puff.

"I thought sure you guessed when I told you to be sure to be back here by 9:30."

I shook my head.

"So are you going to open your presents first? Or do you want cake?"

What I want is for my wish to come true, I thought. But I reached for one of the packages and started opening it. I had to blink a lot because I felt just the slightest bit teary. I hadn't gotten a birthday card from home and I had been feeling kind of forgotten. Now with all the cake and confetti and people, I was overwhelmed.

A little later I sat in the middle of a bunch of crumpled paper and ribbon and surveyed my presents—a Blake College mug, a sweatshirt that said Bop 'til You Drop (from Elaine), a pair of stockings with clocks embroidered at the ankle, a box of Godiva chocolates, a secondhand copy of *Everything You Ever Wanted to Know about Sex but Were Afraid to Ask,* a hand-knit pair of large booties for cold evenings ("I dropped a stitch or two," said Carol, "but I don't think they're going to come unraveled or anything"), and a one-cup coffee pot.

"This was so sweet of you all," I began.

"Wait a minute," said James, producing a package. "I kept this until last because it's delicate. Open it very gently."

It was a very light package for its size. I set it on the floor and began undoing the ribbon and paper. The white box inside had a series of round holes punched in the top. I lifted the top just a little, not sure of what I would find.

"My gawd, it's a lizard!" someone exclaimed.

It was a beautiful small lizard, as shimmering and green as a living jewel. I lifted it out very gently and let it perch on the back of my hand, watching its tongue dart out. The soft skin on its side moved gently as it breathed.

"It's beautiful," I whispered.

"Don't you have to feed them flies?" asked Carol.

"But I'll let it go, of course. I won't have to feed it. I don't think it would be happy in a dorm room."

"Don't you think we could put it back in its box now?" Enid said nervously. "I mean, if it got away we'd have a heck of a time finding it. Imagine waking up with it walking across your nose."

I gently laid it back in the box and put the top on. "I'll take it out to the patio tomorrow. Thank you, James. It's the loveliest birthday present I've ever gotten."

He rubbed his nose self-consciously. "It's not easy finding a present for somebody who's nonmaterialistic."

Dennis was removing the candles from the cake. "Who wants a piece with an icing rose? Here, you take this first piece, Ann."

"Not me, thank you," she said. "I'm trying to cut back."

Everything looked a little blurry through my tears and I had to wipe my eyes on my sleeve and blink some more.

"You take the piece with the roses, Dusty," said Enid. "You need to keep up your strength."

"I'm fine. I'm great. This is the nicest birthday I've ever had! Honestly."

The next day, James came over to the dorm after lunch for the ceremonial release of the lizard. I had found the perfect spot. Mrs. Carmichael, the complex advisor, had made a rock garden in the far corner of the back patio where she grew cactus and funny-looking gray-leaved plants—plants that suited her personality. I lifted the lizard gently out of its box and put it down on a piece of sandstone. I had expected it to dart away at once, but it didn't, so James and I lay on the grass on our stomachs and watched it. I could see the skin of its throat pulsing. It gave a hooded reptilian blink and the sun shimmered on its green back.

"It's sunning itself," I whispered.

"Do you really like it, Dusty?" James asked. "I was afraid you would think it was a little weird."

"I love it. It was a perfect present."

The lizard looked at us, blinked, then dashed away like a flash of green light. It was as if he had never been there. I almost wondered if I had imagined him.

"Maybe he'll stick around in the neighborhood and sun himself on the rocks at the middle of the day again sometime," said James.

I sighed. "Even if I never see him again, it was perfect."

James touched his finger to my lips. "I'm glad you had a nice birthday," he whispered.

It was a few days after that I got a birthday card from home signed by Mom, Dad, and all the kids. I propped it up on my dresser. Days went by that I didn't even think about my family. But when I looked at the birthday card those names scrawled on it could bring home back to me as vividly as if I had stepped into a time machine—the drone of the television, the faint click of silverware in the kitchen, the popsicle wrappers adhering to the sole of my shoe, sticky, knee-high hugs from the boys. It was hard for me to grasp that two such different ways of life as home and school could be contained in the same universe. Sometimes I found myself turning my two different lives over in my mind with a sense of wonder, trying to make sense of it all.

Saturday night, I noticed Enid was getting all dressed up. "Some friends of Rice's are having a party," she explained as she put on her pearl earrings, "and I said I'd go."

"On campus?"

"No. It's in town. I doubt if it will be much fun, but I just want to get out and see people. I don't complain to Dennis because there's nothing he can do about it—his father really needs the help at the restaurant—but the truth is I do get tired of sitting around every single weekend."

After she left, I studied. At midnight, I got in bed and turned out the lights. I had trouble falling asleep, though. Enid had never come in after midnight before and I was worried.

When I finally did fall asleep, I had bad dreams. But I seemed to be standing aside watching my dreams from a slight distance. I suppose I wasn't very deeply asleep. All at once I sat up in bed, wide awake. The luminous dial on Enid's clock radio read 3:00 and her bed was empty. I felt restless with uneasiness. Then I heard a tap on the window. I jumped up out of bed and looked out the window. Enid was standing below, foreshortened and only faintly lit with the dorm's outside lights shining on her fair hair. I flicked our light switch twice just to let her know that I was up and had gotten her signal. Then I put on the slippers Carol had knitted me and crept out into the deserted hallway. The halls were always lit at night so it was no problem to make my way downstairs to the fire door.

I had a momentary qualm as I pushed the fire door open, wondering what I would do if the figure below turned out not to be Enid after all, but she was standing there waiting and popped inside instantly. "Thank goodness. I was afraid I wasn't going to be able to wake you."

"Are you okay?"

"I guess."

I could tell she was limping.

"My heel broke off," she said. "These shoes weren't cheap, either."

"Shhh," I said.

We made our way as quietly as we could back to the room. Enid took off her shoes and sat on the bed.

"What happened?" I asked. "I was worried about you."

"It was awful. I was at this party. I didn't know anybody. It was boring, so I didn't have anything to do but drink. I guess I really had too much because the fact is I really don't remember everything that happened. There are these blank spots, you know? But at one point it suddenly hit me that Rice was trying to get me drunk so he could hit on me. He knows that I don't feel that way about him, but he must have figured if he got me drunk it would be different. He kept filling up my glass and looking at me funny and filling it up again."

"What did you do?"

"I left. I just wanted to get out of there. I wasn't thinking too clearly. I just took off."

"You mean you left on foot, by yourself?"

"Yep. I had a little trouble finding my way. I was sort of confused. But after a while I hit the highway and then I started walking along it."

"Good grief, I'll bet it's ten miles from town and you were in high heels!"

"I think that's when I broke one of them off. It seemed as if I walked forever but finally some boys stopped to picked me up and gave me a ride right back to the dorm. They were about our age and very nice. They asked me if I was all right, but I was pretty upset and I just started crying and couldn't talk. I guess I really did have too much to drink. They asked me if I had been attacked and did I want to go to the police station, and I said no, I was fine, I just need to get back to school, so they took me back here."

For once I was at a loss for words. I was so relieved to have Enid back home safely that I felt positively weak, and when I thought about how much danger she had put herself in I couldn't trust myself to speak. What if those boys hadn't been nice? What if they had been escaped convicts or something? I mean, the danger of what she had done had to be as obvious to her as it was to me. What was the point of rubbing it in? She was lucky to have gotten back alive.

"You know," she said slowly. "I'm beginning to think I have a problem with drinking."

I was afraid to breathe for fear of spoiling the bloom of the moment. This is the real turning around point, I thought. She sees it for herself!

"This blacking out is a bad sign. I know that. I think what I'm going to have to do something. I think I'm going to give up hard liquor."

Give up *hard* liquor? It sank into me slowly that this wasn't quite the turning around point I had hoped for. I felt a sickening thud of disappointment. But what could I do? I couldn't lock her up to keep her away from the stuff.

By Sunday night at seven, my Western Civ. paper was done, so I called James up and asked if he'd like to walk over to Lou's and get a sandwich.

I was kind of down. My problem was that once my mind was free from considering standards of beauty in the Renaissance, it was perfectly free to consider Enid's drinking.

I met James downstairs.

"So you got your paper down early," he said.

"I threw something together."

"You don't have to take that line with me. I know you always make A's."

I looked at him in surprise.

"Well, don't you?"

"How did you know that?"

"Not from you telling me, that's for sure. Did you think I was going to be jealous of your grades or something? I'll have you know I write a pretty decent paper myself, or so I've been told."

"But how did you know I've been getting A's?" I insisted.

"Word gets around."

"I don't see how." I had taken pains to avoid showing my grades to anybody. They didn't fit with Dusty's image. "Are you getting information from some teaching assistant or something?" I asked suspiciously.

"Better than that," he said. "Or worse, depending

on how you look at it. Professor Stuart is my father."

I looked at him blankly. "Are you sure?"

He laughed.

"I mean, I'm just so surprised, that's all."

"Well, I figured you were going to have to find out eventually."

"I don't see what the big secret is. I would think you'd be glad to be Professor Stuart's son."

"Oh, come on, Dusty. Would you want to go to school practically nose to nose with one of your parents?"

"Maybe not. But if you feel that way about it, why didn't you go somewhere else to school?"

"Free tuition is one of the fringe benefits my dad gets. I didn't have a choice. What I hate is that everybody on the faculty knows me. I just try to keep a low profile wherever possible, and I keep counting the days until I can get away to graduate school."

"I guess I can understand that."

We walked over to Lou's and ordered a couple of hot pastrami sandwiches. It was funny but I had gotten to where I had no appetite at dinner. I mean, salisbury steak and fried fish and meat loaf in tomato sauce all repelled me, but the minute I stepped into Lou's I was ravenous.

After I had staved off hunger with a few healthy bites of my sandwich, I broached the subject that was bothering me. "James, I have this sort of a problem I need to talk about. I have this friend, you see, and I'm starting to think this friend of mine has a drinking problem."

Suddenly, he looked grave. "What makes you think that?"

"I may be all wrong, of course, but every night this person has a drink or two before going to bed. What do you think of that?"

"Probably not a good idea."

"I was afraid you would say that. And the other thing is that this person drinks on other occasions, too, and what really worries me is that lately this person has taken to blacking out, not always remembering what happened. Do you think that might be a bad sign?"

"I would say it's a very bad sign."

I sighed. "I had a feeling you would think that. I had this bad feeling about it myself. Tell me this—do you think this person could maybe solve the problem by giving up hard liquor?"

"Extremely doubtful. I mean, it's the alcohol that's the addiction, if you get me. Alcohol in any form is going to be a problem. From what you're telling me, this person ought not to be even breathing the fumes of the stuff."

"I am really worried. I'm not sure this person can handle this problem."

"It's a very big problem. She needs help."

I looked up at him quickly. "I didn't say it was a she."

"It's a guy, then?"

"I can't say who it is."

"Look, Dusty, just tell me one thing. This person isn't Rice MacEnroe is it?"

"Good grief no! I mean, he may be a first-class drunk as far as I know, but who cares? I mean, I know we ought to be concerned about all our fellow

111

human beings, but I sort of draw the line at Rice MacEnroe. Why are you bringing him up?" I looked at him curiously. "I have the feeling you don't believe me when I tell you I can't stand him." I thought about it a minute. "And actually really nothing could be easier to believe if you've ever met him."

"Well, you're not exactly being candid with me right now, are you?"

"I am being as candid as I can be."

"Look," he said heavily. "This friend of yours had better get himself/herself to Alcoholics Anonymous."

"But you know, this person is coping pretty well. Don't you think that for this alcohol thing to be a serious problem it has to be affecting a person's work or relationships with other people? I seem to remember reading that somewhere."

"This person is kidding herself, if she thinks that."

"Or himself," I added quickly.

"Yes. Kidding himself or herself."

"I had a feeling you were going to say that."

"That's because deep down you know I'm right."

"Maybe so." I didn't see how on earth I could get Enid to go to an Alcoholics Anonymous meeting. From the beginning we had established a pattern on noninterference in each other's lives. After all, nobody wants to get away from home only to be mothered by her roommate. I wouldn't even know how to begin bringing the subject up.

James squeezed my hands. "Recognizing the problem is the first big step," he said.

"I'm not so sure about that," I said doubtfully.

Chapter Nine

Classes were scheduled for the Friday after Thanksgiving, so nobody went home for the holiday. A lot of people were upset about this, but not I. A Thanksgiving card from my family, white tablecloths on the cafeteria tables and cafeteria-style turkey and dressing—that was plenty enough Thanksgiving for me. In fact, I figured that not having to go home was one of the things I had to be thankful about.

Then, not long after Thanksgiving, I got a letter from Mom.

Dear Deborah Susan,

I'm sorry it's been so long since I've written but we've had a lot on our minds. Things have been very tense at your father's work, going from bad to worse. And Friday, they fired him!

Of course, it was a dreadful shock after all those years he has worked at the hardware store. At least, he was not the only one to suffer so he doesn't have to feel it was his fault. They fired all the old staff. I can see now that they just kept them on long enough to be sure they really understood how the business operated and then they wanted to move in their own people.

Your father did get a month's severance pay and he is also eligible for unemployment but that is more or less a drop in the bucket. We cleaned out the bank account in order to buy a nice suit since your father can hardly go job hunting in what he has. Self-confidence is so important when you are interviewing and, naturally, he is not feeling very self-confident after all that has happened. I'm sure that with all his experience he will be able to find a new job. It is a little worrisome that the paper mill has just shut down and the job market locally is depressed, but as I tell him, qualified people who are willing to work hard can always find something. We are not downhearted! Don't worry about us.

Love,
Mom

"Would you watch where you're going?" a guy snapped at me. I dimly remembered bumping up against him before, but right then I was too much in my own private misery to worry about apologizing. I just wanted to go lie in a darkened room someone and try to calm down. What was going to become of my family? I was hit by fear so strong it was a physical sensation. Where would my father find another job? Wasn't this the way that people who were already barely scraping by ended up on the streets, homeless, like those people on the evening news?

"Are you okay?" James was holding onto my arm. I hadn't even noticed him coming up.

"I feel kind of sick, actually," I gulped.

"Infirmary kind of sick? Or sit-down-for-a-minute kind of sick?"

"Maybe I'll just get a cup of coffee or something."

He led me in the direction of the union. "You look awful. Are you sure you're okay?"

I smiled wanly and nodded. He deposited me in a booth in the union and came back in a minute with two cups of coffee.

He shot me a keen glance. "Problems at home?"

For a split second I seriously considered coming out and saying that my father had lost his job. But at the last minute I couldn't go through with it. I had the feeling that if I let that part of my life through it might suck up and destroy everything I had built for myself, all the little bits of happiness and security and love I had collected since September.

"I really don't want to talk about it. It wouldn't make it any better."

He put his arm around me, and I leaned my head on his shoulder. I had never realized before how important it was not to feel alone.

"Walk you back to the dorm?"

"Okay."

A brisk wind was blowing in from the bay and a couple of enterprising guys had gotten out their skateboards. It was a simple matter then to throw out a sheet to catch the wind and then to sail to class on the skateboard.

"Looks like fun, doesn't it?" said James.

The skateboarders did look indecently happy. "My father lost his job," I said in a wooden voice. "The company he worked for was bought out."

"Oh." James looked at me. "There is such a thing as unemployment compensation, you know."

"I know that. But it's not much money."

"Is he looking for another job now?"

I nodded.

"Well, he'll probably find one."

I realized that James had no feel at all for what it was like to live close to the margin of survival. His family probably had lots of money in the bank and no outstanding bills.

"Are you worried this may mean you'll have to drop out of school?"

"No. I'm on scholarship."

"That's good anyway."

"Yep," I said glumly. "One less mouth to feed at home."

I was already wishing I hadn't told him. It made it all seem more real somehow. And telling him meant the troubles of my old life were infiltrating the new one. They weren't completely separate anymore.

"I'm sorry," he said softly.

I could feel my throat closing up and I was afraid I was going to cry. I ran inside quickly.

After getting Mom's letter, I had a lot of trouble sleeping. I would lie in bed staring at the dark ceiling, stiff from head to toe. I felt as if I were falling from a great height. I didn't have any rational thoughts, just incoherent fear. What will happen? What will happen to them? The questions kept going through my mind like a scratched record.

And yet by daylight, there were times I was able to forget about my family completely. James, with a tact I really appreciated, never mentioned what I had told him. Sometimes I would catch him shooting me a concerned look, but it was as if he realized I had to keep a fence around my feelings by not talking about the problems at home.

Around me, life went on as usual. People complained about the cafeteria food, hung their panty hose on the shower curtain rod to dry, and generally acted revoltingly normal. And, of course, there were the dorm meetings.

"What does this mean?" I asked Carol. I was reading the notice on the door to the dorm about a meeting for all the dorms in our complex. "Is it about this ironing business again?" I asked.

"No, just official announcements by Mrs. Carmichael about exam scheduling, holiday procedures and that sort of thing."

"Couldn't they just send it to us on ditto sheets? And what's this about attendance being 'compulsory'?"

Carol shrugged. She had that "official" look on her face so I didn't bother to ask any more questions. I knew if I did I would only get the standard administration line. I was really beginning to wonder about that meeting. What was the big secret?

That night I was standing in front of the bathroom mirror carefully retouching my dark roots when I saw Elaine come in and start emptying a bottle of gin in the bathtub.

I stared at her. "Is this some new beauty bath or something? Because I hate to tell you but you forgot to put the plug in the tub. The stuff is all running out."

"Very funny," she said. "You saw the notice about the complex meeting didn't you? Well, you know what 'compulsory attendance' means. It means they're going to search the rooms for liquor."

"Are you serious?"

She held up the empty gin bottle. "Do I look like I'm kidding around?"

I rushed back to the room, but there was no sign of Enid. It seemed an eternity before she came in.

"At last!" I exploded. "Where have you been?"

She held out her left hand and beamed at me. "Dennis and I are engaged."

"Congratulations," I said curtly. I wasted no time filing her in on what Elaine had told me. I knew that those bottles of booze were still under her bed. "I think we'd better go in right now and pour it all out. We can put the bottles in a carry-all to get them to the shower. You'd better wear your shower cap so you look more convincing. Hurry up, we don't have much time."

"But I've got eight bottles under there!"

"It's a lot, but with both of us working on it, I think we can probably get them all poured out in just a few minutes. And I think if anybody on our own floor saw us, they probably wouldn't turn us in anyway."

"But I don't want to pour them all out!"

"Weren't you going to give up hard liquor?"

"It just seems so wasteful! That stuff is expensive."

"Do you want us both to get thrown out of school?"

"Wait a minute," she said. "I have a better idea."

I could hardly believe it, but only moments later, I was gingerly carrying a heavy typewriter case full of liquor bottles out of our room. I had the case pressed against my stomach and I was trying hard to keep it level. The last thing I wanted was for the bottles to go clink. *This* was her better idea?

"We can put it all in Sue Ellen's car," whispered Enid. "She never locks her trunk. I'll go first because it might look suspicious if we both went out at once. I'll meet you in the parking lot." She hoisted her typewriter case and headed downstairs. I got the horrors just thinking of how she was having to walk through the den of the honor court justices downstairs.

Only a couple of minutes later, I was going downstairs myself, my heart pounding. Luckily, I met no one in the downstairs hall. I pushed the dorm door open with my hip and edged myself carefully outside onto the patio.

The night was cool and foggy, but even so, several couples were hanging around the gate saying prolonged goodnights. Margaret Wentworth and a baby-faced boy I didn't know were standing right by the gate. That was bad. I only hoped Margaret was sufficiently involved in what she was saying that she would not notice me as I squeezed past her.

No such luck.

"Why, Deborah Susan!" she cried.

I jumped and the bottles inside the typewriter case clinked.

"Excuse me," she said contritely. "I mean Dusty. I keep forgetting."

I managed a travesty of a smile. I felt as if my knees might buckle.

"Where are you going on such a nasty night?" She looked down at the typewriter case I was holding.

"I borrowed somebody's typewriter," I said quickly. "And they want it back right away."

"What a coincidence. I just saw your roommate going by with a typewriter, too."

"Yes. We were typing a duet. Excuse me, please."

She stepped back, but as I walked past her, the bottles gave distinct clink. I squeezed my eyes shut and just kept going. After I had gone fifteen steps or so, I was able to breathe more easily. She had not run after me.

By the time I got to the parking lot, I was panting, whether with anxiety or with hurrying I couldn't be sure. Enid was standing under a light next to a green Volkswagen, a typewriter case at her feet.

"I've already put my bottles in the trunk," she said. "Come on, let's get the rest of them in."

I glanced around anxiously. Then I opened the case and moved the bottles from the typewriter case into Sue Ellen's trunk. I laid them one by one next to the tire iron. Enid slammed the trunk shut.

"I really do appreciate this, Dusty. You don't have to worry about another thing now. I'll give Rice a call and he can take care of them. Maybe we can work something out where I can trade all these for a few bottles of wine and a six-pack or something."

We walked back toward the dorm, shoulders hunched against the chilly fog.

"I didn't know you were still speaking to Rice," I said.

"Oh, I don't know. I guess I went off the deep end a little bit that night I had too much to drink. Maybe I was getting paranoid and imagining things. Rice said he went looking for me and was really worried about me."

"I'll bet," I muttered.

"I'm afraid Rice may have gotten the wrong idea. He doesn't seem to accept that we're just drinking buddies."

"Maybe you ought to stop seeing him altogether," I said promptly. "You don't want to lead him on."

"I was thinking the same thing. When I call him about the liquor, I'll tell him that we've got to talk. I can't go drinking with him now that I'm engaged to Dennis. If Dennis ever found out about it he'd have a fit."

When we got to the dorm a student assistant was swinging the patio gates closed.

Girls were already coming down to the complex lounge for the dorm meeting. Enid and I went on into the lounge. Mrs. Carmichael was standing next to the television a permanent sour look on her face. She waited for a while, then called roll to make sure everyone in the complex was either present or accounted for. Then she began to read the announcements. It took over a half-hour for her to get through them and the whole time I had the impression she was dragging her feet, and stalling for time. Of course, that was not proof that the dorm rooms were being searched, but it seemed to suggest that. It was unbelievably easy to imagine teams of spies scouring the closets of our rooms and peering under our beds while she droned on about the final exam schedule. Enid and I had had a narrow squeak all right. What if I hadn't seen Elaine pouring out that bottle in the bathroom and found out what was going on? I didn't even like to think about it.

Finally, the meeting was over. As we were all filing out of the lounge, Elaine spotted the ring on Enid's finger. "You're engaged!" she shrieked.

I had almost forgotten about that little detail.

Enid smiled happily. "We're going to get married this summer and then I'll transfer to Florida State and finish up there. Dennis has already been accepted at grad school there."

"I'm so happy for you," Ann said.

"Dennis is a sweetheart," said Elaine. "You're a lucky woman."

"Dennis is lucky, too," I put in. But when I thought about all those bottles of booze, I wasn't so sure.

The next morning, at breakfast, James buttered a muffin and announced that he was not at all surprised that Dennis and Enid were engaged.

"I know, I know. You saw it from the beginning," I said.

"No, but I can see which way the wind is blowing when Dennis sits around making up budgets and checking on the transfer requirements at Florida State."

He seemed to see that I was not that bubbly about the whole thing because he added kindly, "Of course, it's tough for you, losing a roommate."

I nodded. I certainly couldn't tell James my worries about Enid's drinking since he was one of Dennis's closest friends.

"I'm going to have to cut Hopkins's class tomorrow afternoon," James said, "but I think he's just going to review for the final and I'm solid in there so it's okay. I'm buying a loft from a guy over at South Florida and I'm going to spend tomorrow afternoon carting it over from the South Florida campus. It's all disassembled and I think I can get it in my Mom's station wagon if I leave the back open. The beams are going to stick out quite a bit, of course."

"Are you sure it's going to be safe?" I asked. "What if it fell down when you were up there and you got a concussion or something?" The words were no sooner out of my mouth than I realized how much I sounded like the old, nervous Deborah Susan. While this was hardly surprising considering the shocks my nervous system had suffered lately, I hated to hear the querulous sound in my voice.

James didn't seem to notice. He was finishing off his square of cake. "Believe me, it's going to be solid as a rock. The beams are really thick. I got the guy to get up on the thing himself and jump around before I said I'd buy it. When I get it all put up, you'll have to come over and see it."

Only iron self-control kept me from suggesting that a building inspector should check the thing out first. These days it was getting harder and harder for me to maintain a carefree facade.

I didn't really expect to see James Friday night because I knew he was going to be busy assembling his loft. He didn't even show up at supper. I went to the library and put in a couple of hours studying hard for finals.

When I came back from the library, I spotted

Rice and Enid walking out toward the fill. It was dark and I couldn't see them that clearly, but I had the impression Rice was carrying a blanket and a six-pack. I wondered if Enid had succeeded in making it perfectly clear the nature of the serious talk.

"Dusty!" James trotted toward me coming from the other direction, skidded to a stop and waved a paper in my face.

"Your history paper? Let me see." I grabbed at it. "I thought you were going to be working on that loft all afternoon."

"It's all done. Some of the guys helped me. And Andy Henkle picked up my paper at Hopkins's class."

"An A!"

"Yeah, and you know Hopkins. Every A he gives away it's like it was his firstborn child."

"Neat. That is really fantastic!"

"Just let me read you his comment. 'Well-organized and original. Good use of sources. Altogether fine work. Your diction is not, however, always as precise as it could be.' " He made a face. "He's always got to get a dig in. Nothing is ever perfect."

"But that's wonderful! I'll bet this is the only A he gave out, isn't it?"

"Might be," he said smugly. "Want to come see the loft now?"

We passed a couple of disheveled guys on the way over to James's dorm. With finals drawing near, the standards of personal grooming around campus had sunk to new lows. In every dorm were people who were subsisting solely on black coffee and peanut butter sandwiches, trying to do a semester's studying in a matter of days. There was a faint undercurrent of hysteria everywhere. Even Carol had been without makeup the last time I had seen her. But the creepiest thing was the quiet. In normal times, heavy metal music blared in James's dorm, the occasional stray basketball thudded against a wall, weight lifting equipment landed on the floor, and some guy seemed to be invariably calling to another down the stairs. "Hey, Grogan, what happened to that tie I lent you?" Tonight was different. Tonight the only sound I could hear was water running in the bathroom.

I had been in James's rooms before but in the unearthly quiet of exam time it seemed different. More private.

We gazed up at the loft.

"Isn't it something?" he said.

"Amazing. You really do have a lot more space this way."

"Go ahead. Climb on up the ladder."

I hesitated.

"It's perfectly safe. We bolted it on. Go ahead."

I climbed up. There was not a lot of space left over in the loft once the bed had been put up there, but I had to admit it had a very nice cozy feel.

"Like it?"

"I adore it."

"Hang on. I'm coming up."

I cringed as he climbed up the ladder and flopped down on the mattress beside me, but it didn't collapse.

"I told you it was strong, didn't I? The guy who owned it before weighed 250 pounds and he told me he had orgies on it all the time."

"A likely story."

"Yeah, well, maybe he did exaggerate a little bit. He told me he planned a career in sales."

"That part I believe."

He put his arm around me and drew me close. "The only trouble with this thing is there isn't a lot of room up here."

"It's true. You'd have to really like each other to share a loft like this."

"Well, it works out for us, doesn't it? Since we really like each other, I mean."

He put both arms around me. When we kissed, I seemed to lose my bearings. It was as if we were on a faraway planet, spinning alone in a dark universe. Finally, I pulled away from him and licked my dry lips. "I think I'd better go now," I said hastily.

I rolled off the bed and began climbing backward down the ladder.

"Hey wait a minute. I'm coming, too."

"It really is a super loft," I said. "And congratulations on your A." I rested my hands on his chest for a second and smiled at him. We looked at each other a minute, not saying anything.

"It really is a neat loft, isn't it?"

"It really is."

"Dusty, I think I love you, and I'm not just saying that to get you up in the loft with me."

"I know."

He hesitated. "So—what are you thinking?"

What I was really thinking was that I wished he would call me Deborah Susan. I was having the sensation again that I was in a video of somebody else's life and this was one time I wanted everything to seem real.

Just then a skinny boy burst into the room. His hair was wet and sticking out in spikes and he looked frantic. "James! I can't get Scott to answer his door."

James swore. "Exams. I hate them. Wait a minute and I'll get a passkey."

"I'm going now," I said.

James nodded absently as he dashed out.

As I was leaving the dorm, I heard somebody shrieking, "Well, how was I supposed to know you were sleeping? Whoever heard of anybody sleeping at eight o'clock?"

So the missing guy had only been sleeping. I was glad nothing had been wrong after all. I pulled on my jacket and walked back toward my dorm feeling warm inside. My birthday wish had come true. What a lucky thing that I had been able to blow out eighteen candles at a single puff.

Out over the water I could see headlights passing over the Skyway Bridge. At this distance they looked better than the stars.

Suddenly I spotted Rice MacEnroe striding back alone from the fill. He was wearing a white sweatshirt so I could make him out even in the dim light. I stared in that direction, straining my eyes at first. But there was no doubt about it. It was Rice, all right. A minute later, he passed within twenty feet of me, light spilling onto him from the dorms. I could see then that he was angry.

Enid has told him off, I thought. Good. She ought to be coming along any minute now herself.

I sat down on the planter outside the dorm and waited for her, but there was no sign of her. A couple in hooded sweatshirts came in dragging a blanket and holding a bottle of wine, but neither of them was Enid.

I was getting cold, but I didn't go in. I glanced at my watch. I was beginning to be uneasy. Was it really likely that Enid would sit out on the sea wall on a night like this drinking beer by herself?

My teeth began to chatter from the cold. She was out there, presumably alone, on the fill and on a night so chilly that no one could possibly want to sit looking at the stars. Something had to have gone wrong.

I ran all the way to James's dorm, dashed inside and banged on his door.

"What's wrong?" he said as soon as he saw my face.

"Do you have a good strong flashlight?"

"There's one in Mom's car."

"Can I borrow it?"

"What for, Dusty? What's wrong?"

I hesitated. But it was pretty clear to me that if something was wrong I was going to need help. And I would be just as glad to have company when I went out on the fill. "I'm afraid something has happened to Enid. She went out on the fill and she hasn't come back."

"Are you sure? What would she be doing out there?"

"Would you come with me to look for her?"

"Sure. Come on."

James got the flashlight out of his mother's car and we trotted off in the direction of the fill.

"It's going to be like looking for a needle in a haystack. There are miles of sea wall. What makes you so sure she's out there?

"I saw her go. I have a rough idea of the direction she went in."

To my relief he did not ask any more questions about what she was doing out there. I certainly didn't want to have to tell him she had gone out on the fill with Rice. It sounded so cheap.

Walking on the soft sand of the fill was not easy. A couple of times I had the sensation I was going to sink in up to my knees.

"It just seems so crazy," James muttered, playing the flashlight on the sand ahead of us. "Why would she come out here?"

"She told me she wanted to have a private talk with somebody," I said.

He darted a sharp look at me, but I pretended not to see it.

Suddenly I thought I heard something. I took the flashlight and shone it in the direction of the sound. "Over there," I said. "Let's go that way."

A minute later, when we had almost reached the sea wall, the flashlight fell on something I couldn't quite make out. We rushed closer, shining the flashlight until it fell on a figure that seemed to be doubled over.

"Enid!" I cried, running over to her.

"I am so sick," she moaned. "I've been throwing up."

James played the flashlight around us and I saw the bright glitter of the glass of the beer bottles in the six-pack. It looked to me as if half of them still had the caps on.

"Did you have too much to drink?" I asked.

"I hardly had anything to drink," she protested, bending over with a groan. "I'm so dizzy."

"Do you think you can stand up?" James asked absently. He was playing the flashlight nervously over the sand.

"I don't know," she said.

Then she slumped over on the blanket.

"I think she's passed out!" I cried. "Enid!"

"She's fainted," said James abruptly. "Get out of the way, Dusty. I'll get her."

I moved out of his way. "I'll get the beer and the blanket," I said.

"Forget about them," said James. He scooped Enid up awkwardly in his arms. "You just get the flashlight. We're going to the hospital."

"To the hospital?" I took the flashlight from him. "James, I don't like to say this, but I think she's just passed out. Once or twice before she has drunk a little too much. I think if we just get her back to the room—" I trotted after him.

"Maybe so," he said. "But I think we'd better have a doctor look at her. I can't be a hundred percent sure, but it looked to me as if maybe she had thrown up a little blood. That's what it looked like to me."

"I think she's coming to," I said.

"I feel so dizzy," she murmured.

"Hang on," said James. "We're going to get you taken care of."

Luckily, Enid was not heavy. But still, I could see that carrying her over the sand was no picnic, and by the time we had gone half way, James was panting heavily. We stayed close to the sea wall as far as we could because the sand was somewhat firmer at the edge. We passed a couple who were making out but I hardly noticed them. I was concentrating on

130

shining the flashlight directly in James's path so he could be sure of keeping his footing.

"Lucky thing I've got the station wagon," he said, as at last he tottered off the fill and onto the solid footing of grass. "We can just pile her in and drive her over to the hospital."

"Do you really think this could be serious?" My voice sounded quavery.

"I don't have any idea."

Enid was fully conscious by the time we were strapping her in the back seat of the station wagon, but when I told her we were going to the hospital, she didn't protest, which told me as much as anything about how sick she felt.

I sat in the back seat with her while James drove. Light flickered on Enid's pale face as we sped toward the hospital. Her hands felt cold. I kept telling myself that we were lucky James knew the way to the hospital, we were lucky he happened to have his mother's car, and we were lucky that I had happened to see Rice coming back from the fill. But counting your blessings on the way to the hospital is a pretty melancholy business.

At last I saw a white light that said "Emergency." James drove back to the parking lot behind the hospital and parked near the sign. I got out and he helped me get Enid out of the car.

"Can you walk?" I asked her.

"Oh, sure," she said. But her voice was faint.

"Hold onto her, Dusty. Look, hang onto us, Enid. We can't risk you passing out on the concrete here. You could get hurt."

We supported her as we made our way from the parking lot to the entrance. At the glass doors of the entrance light spilled out onto the sidewalk. An orderly rolled an empty stretcher past us. Incongruously, he was humming a tune.

Enid was white in the face and a little unsteady, but at least she was conscious. We went inside and sat down in the plastic shell seats of the waiting room. The other people in the waiting room were in their undershirts, their torn jeans and their old pajamas and none of them looked too cheerful. The emergency room is definitely a come-as-you-are kind of party, I thought. I held Enid's hand and tried to keep from shivering.

We had to wait a long time. People left the waiting room and came back with cardboard cups of coffee. A little kid whimpered and rubbed his eyes.

Finally, someone told us it was Enid's turn. She went in by herself and we settled in to do some more waiting.

James leaned over with his arms dangling, his elbows resting on his thighs, a picture of fatigue. "So is Enid your friend with the drinking problem?"

"Yes."

"Well, I'm glad to hear that. I was afraid it might be you."

"Me? I don't drink!"

"I didn't think so, but you were being so super mysterious, you had me kind of worried."

I had a good reason for that, I thought.

We waited some more and still Enid didn't come out. I don't know how long we waited out there, but it seemed forever, as if we had died and gone to a hell with eye-rest green walls.

At last I heard quiet footsteps on the tile and a woman in white came over to us. "We're going to have to admit your friend," she said. "You might want to go in and see if she'd like you to bring any of her things to the hospital tomorrow."

"Is she all right? What's the matter with her?"

"It looks like an ulcer. She's had some bleeding from it. That's why she fainted."

"Is she going to be all right?"

"I think so. There's not a great deal of bleeding. We'll have to keep her for a few days though."

I followed the woman into a white room. Then she went off. Enid was lying on a stainless steel table, her face bleached by the fluorescent lights. Her ankles and forearms were frosted with the fine sand from the fill but she didn't seem to notice. She managed a faint smile.

"Looks like you're going to miss exams," I said.

"That's all right. How did you and James ever find me out there, Dusty?"

"I saw Rice coming back without you, so we just went in that direction."

"When I got sick he was pretty mad."

I didn't think it was necessary to comment on Rice's behavior. If Enid couldn't see the kind of guy he was by now, she was worse off than I thought.

"Are you going to need anything? They said you'd have to stay for a few days."

"A toothbrush, I guess. A nightgown. Whatever you think."

It was pretty clear she didn't have much strength. After a while, an orderly helped her get off the table and into a wheelchair. She looked very small as they rolled her away.

I went back to James in the waiting room. "I

have to come back tomorrow to bring her toothbrush and stuff."

He stood up. "And I've got to call Dennis."

I grabbed at his arm. "You aren't going to tell
him!"

He gently removed my hand. "You think I can
drive Enid to the hospital and not tell Dennis she's
there? You must be out of your mind."

"Yes, but you're not going to tell him—all of it,
are you?"

He didn't answer me. We walked on outside and
stood under the white light that said "Emergency."

"Well, are you?" I repeated.

"Maybe he won't ask," he said finally.

Chapter Ten

The next day, James drove me to the hospital to visit Enid. She was in a semi-private room with a white screen between her bed and the other bed in the room. A large vase of red carnations was on her bedside table.

"Dennis was here a minute ago," she said. "You just missed him."

"How do you feel?" I asked. I perched on the edge of a chair and regarded her anxiously.

"Pretty awful, actually," she said. "You know, it turns out I have an ulcer. Can you believe that? My father had ulcers, so I guess I shouldn't be all that surprised. The doctor told me it runs in families. I talked to him this morning and he gave me this list of what I can have and what I can't have. I'm going to have to be very careful. Goodbye pizza, and no more booze in any way shape or form."

"Do you think you're going to be able to stick to that?" I asked, my eyes fixed on her face.

"You think I want to end up like this all over again?" she shuddered. "Believe me, I do not."

I believed her.

Later when James and I were driving home, I

said, "This might turn out to be a blessing in disguise."

"If she sticks to it."

"I think she will. Particularly with Rice out of the way."

"What was this business with her and Rice, anyway?"

"Rice, a.k.a. the Prince of Darkness," I said bitterly. "He was always trying to get Enid to drink. They were drinking buddies pure and simple, but I think he had other ambitions."

"Well, he didn't pour the stuff down her throat, Dusty."

I sighed heavily. "What difference does it make whose fault it was? It's all over."

"Maybe so, but it gives me the creeps to think of Dennis walking into a situation like not having any idea what's going on."

"But she's going to quit drinking!"

"Yeah, but . . ." His voice trailed off, but I could tell he was unhappy.

I played what I thought was my strongest card. "I may be wrong," I said hesitantly, "but I don't think Dennis would thank you for telling him. You know he can't see reason on the subject of drinking. If you say anything to him, it's going to smash everything between him and Enid. Do you really think that's what he wants?"

James's lips were tight and we drove back to the dorm in silence.

All the next day, people kept popping in to see me and ask how Enid was getting along. I tried to give the impression she had been taken ill suddenly in the room the night before. I certainly didn't want to go into all the grisly details about Rice and the fill and everything. My instincts told me that James wasn't in any hurry to rush to Dennis with the story. I thought I had a fairly good chance of keeping the whole thing quiet.

With so much on my mind, it was hard for me to concentrate on studying. I was about to put away my books and call it quits when Ann burst into the room.

"Hide me!" she whispered. "Meg is looking for me."

I opened my closet and pushed the clothes to one side. Ann stepped in and I slid the closet closed. There was a knocking at the door to my room. Cautiously I stuck my head out. I was careful not to swing the door wide open because didn't want Meg to get the idea she was being invited in.

"Have you seen Annie?" she asked, her lips pouting a little.

"No, she's not here." I heard the metallic rattle of hangers in my closet and had to cough to cover the noise. "Have you tried Carol's room?" I said quickly. "She might have gone over there to borrow something."

"I looked there. She wasn't there, either." Meg looked down at the huge slice of coconut cake she was carrying on a paper plate. "I brought some cake for her and now I can't find her anywhere."

"That's too bad. Maybe you ought to just eat it yourself. Look, I hate to run you off, Meg, but I've really got to hit the books."

She pushed her hair out of her face and smiled her little triangular smile. "Well, if you see her . . ."

"Sure. Sure. I'll tell her you're looking for her."

I closed the door and waited until I heard Meg's footsteps going down the hall.

I went over and opened the closet. "You can come out. She's gone."

"Are you sure? Oh, thank you, Dusty, thank you, thank you. I won't forget this. I know I must look crazy, but I just couldn't stand it a minute longer. I had to get away from her."

"You don't have to explain to me. I don't see how you've stood her this long."

"Do you mind if I stay in your room just a little while? Until I'm sure she's given up? I'll be real quiet. I know you've got to study."

"Actually, I was about to quit. Sure, stay. I'm kind of lonely with Enid away."

Ann sat cross-legged on Enid's bed. "That's just awful about her being in the hospital. We ought to get together and send her something to let her know we're thinking of her."

"Maybe I ought to get Meg to send her that co-conut cake."

Ann grinned. "It really is unbelievable the way she keeps at it, isn't it? I know she doesn't mean any harm, but she's driving me crazy."

"Sure she means harm. You're probably too tactful with her. When you attack her with a baseball bat, maybe she'll catch on that you mean business."

Ann giggled. "You're good for me, Dusty."

"You want some popcorn?"

"That sounds great, but . . ."

"Without butter, I know. Coming up." I pulled the popper out from the cubbyhole behind Enid's bed and plugged it in. "Ann, when you went away to college did you have this, well, this image of the kind of person you wanted to be?"

"Oh, sure," she said wryly. "I was going to be the beautiful intellectual, didn't you know?"

"So how did it work out?"

"Oh, come on, if it had worked out, you wouldn't have to ask. I had no idea of how stiff the competition was going to be. Carol's the beautiful one and you're the intellectual."

I sighed. "I didn't plan to be the intellectual. I figured I was going to be cool, well-balanced, wholesome, tough, and unflappable."

"Well, you are."

"I don't know. I don't feel very tough right now."

"Look at the way you hid me from Meg!"

She had a point. I supposed it was possible I was more unflappable than I thought.

"I will always think of you as the tough, but wholesome blond intellectual," said Ann with great firmness.

"No kidding?"

"I'm serious. You're just feeling low because Enid is sick."

"I guess so."

Ann peeked out the door. "She's gone. I can't even hear her asking around. She must have given up and gone someplace looking for a boy. Golly, you're a real friend, Dusty."

The next morning at breakfast, I was surprised to see that the sight of bacon and eggs revolted me. The Danishes and doughnuts looked yucky, too. I didn't think it was just exams getting to me. Carol had been right. There was an incredible monotony to the cafeteria food. It wasn't just that they always had bacon and eggs, it was that the bacon and eggs were always exactly the same, the bacon slightly undercooked, the scrambled eggs glistening fat yellow curls in the metal pans under the heat lamps. And I was sure they cooked their orange juice, too. Here we were in the heart of orange country and their orange juice tasted as if it had been powdered and reconstituted. I grabbed a packet of Bran Buds. I certainly had never thought I would end up eating Bran Buds for breakfast, but anything for a change.

As I took my tray to a table, I wondered if I were really tired of the food or if this was the sign of some more sinister kind of existential malaise, the sort of thing we talked about in French class when we were reading Camus. A boy walked past me with a shriveled prune Danish and I shuddered. No, I decided, this is not existential malaise. I am tired of the food.

I sat down and opened my cereal packet.

"Hey look!" someone behind me said. "Get a load of the pump house!"

I glanced out the big window and saw that someone had been up in the night painting on the pump house wall.

"Hebrews 13:8?" I said, puzzled.

"It's a Bible verse," the guy behind me said. "I wonder what it says. We'll have to go back to the dorm and look it up. Hey, write it down on a napkin or something."

James slid into the seat next to me. "I know what it says," he murmured.

"Did you write that?" I said accusing tones. "Were you up skulking around with a paint can, dodging the campus cops?"

"Not I. But I saw it early this morning and I looked it up." He produced a Bible. "It's a comment on the cafeteria food, I believe. Here it is, folks, Hebrews 13:8: 'Jesus Christ, the same yesterday, today and tomorrow.' "

I burst out laughing.

"Hey, let me see that," said the guy behind us.

All over the cafeteria, laughter was beginning to ripple as people pointed to the pump house.

"Exams," said James, grinning. "People get crazy, don't they?"

Enid's mother came the next day to get her. Enid was going home to recover. But the rest of us were knee deep in exams. It was weird. I had expected tension around exam time, but it was more than that. The campus seemed to take on an air of unreality. Maybe it was because nobody had a regular schedule. People were sitting up late at night studying and there were no classes. It was like living in a permanent daze where the only things you did were go to meals, study and fill endless blue books with your essays.

After one of my exams, I went by the mail room and found a letter from Mom. I hadn't heard from her in some time and I tore it open with misgiving.

Dear Deborah Susan,

Your father has a new job! The only catch is that we have to move to Jacksonville, but we don't mind that. Peggy is not too happy about adjusting to the new schools, but the boys are very excited. Must run now and pack.

Love,
Mom

I stared at the letter scarcely grasping it. Dad had a job. It felt like a miracle. I sighed in relief. I couldn't wait to tell James. As I left the mail room, I noticed that the guy I had collided with a couple of times before was pressing himself defensively against the wall and eyeing me with mistrust.

My French exam turned out to hold no surprises and I was fairly confident I came through the calculus exam all right, too. By Wednesday I had only one exam to go. By then, some people were packing their cars and driving home.

Ann and I watched Elaine's Volkswagen, filled with six people, depart for Miami. I was glad I was not one of the passengers. "I have a Thursday afternoon exam," Ann said gloomily. "Isn't that gross? Practically everybody will be gone by then."

"All freshmen have a Thursday exam."

"But the place is already thinning out. It's awful to see people driving away and know that I'm stuck here. I can't fly out until Friday morning. When are you leaving?"

"I'm not sure. My parents are in the middle of moving and with all the confusion, they haven't written me when they're coming. I guess they'll probably come on Friday night or Saturday. They're not too well-organized so it's hard to say."

"I know why you're not in any hurry to get away," said Ann. "It's because of James, isn't it?"

Ann was right, of course. I was not in any hurry to get home. But it wasn't just that James was hanging around until the last day. It was that now, school felt almost like home.

By Friday afternoon, practically no one was left in the dorm. Ann had caught a cab to the airport that morning. The campus was beginning to take on a deserted appearance.

"I'm taking off for home, now," James said when he came over just before supper. "I wanted to give you this first." He handed me a small gold wrapped box topped with a tiny red bow.

"You didn't have to do that," I said.

"But I wanted to."

"Do you want me to open it now?"

"No, I want you to open it on Christmas. That way you'll have something to remind you of me."

"I don't need anything to remind me of you."

"Hey, wait a minute," he grinned, "the correct answer is 'your face is graven on my heart.' "

I smiled. "Yes, that, too."

We kissed then and I could feel myself slipping into another sort of gear, holding on to him as if he were the only thing I was really sure of in the entire world. "My dad's got a new job," I murmured.

James pulled away and beamed at me. "Great. Then everything's perfect, right?"

"Just about."

"And just in time for Christmas."

I stood at my window and watched as he walked back to his dorm, not wanting to let him out of my sight. His red shirt was bright against the buff color of the lawn and the sun picked up the light streaks in his hair. Finally, he turned behind the cafeteria and disappeared from view. A Mazda sped past, a suitcase strapped to its roof. Everyone was going home.

That night, I was one of only a few people who were in the cafeteria for supper. This is good, I told myself. This gives me some time to rest and pull myself together after the rigors of exams before I have to face all the mess at home. After supper, I went back to my room, popped some popcorn and read a mystery story.

The next morning I sat in the lounge with my suitcase, waiting for my parents. They had been late before, lots of times, but this was carrying it to extremes. A maid came through with a pail and a mop and looked at me curiously.

Every time I heard a car I jumped up and ran to the door, but the cars always drove right past. By noon, my nerves were shot. I got change for a dollar from the maid and called home. "The number you have dialed has been disconnected," said the recorded announcement.

It was a bad moment. I went back to my room and rooted around until I found Mom's letter. It was postmarked a week ago. Presumably, then, the number was disconnected not because they had failed to pay the bill, but because they had already moved to Jacksonville. Unfortunately, they had neglected to tell me their new address. Was it really possible that they had moved and left me no way to reach them?

I couldn't think of anything to do but to go back the lounge and sit by my suitcase.

What an irony. I had worked so hard on forgetting about my parents and now they had forgotten about me!

The maid propped the door open with her pail. "I'm going to have to lock up in here as soon as I finish," she said.

I jumped. "Let me make a phone call."

I dialed James's number from the lounge.

"James?" I said, my voice shaking slightly. "This is Dusty. Could I possibly come stay with you? My parents have forgotten to pick me up. They've been moving and I guess in all the confusion they just didn't realize the term was ending. I don't have any way to reach them."

"Hang on," he said. "Just a minute."

I looked over at the maid's pail, wondering what I would do if James's parents weren't prepared to take on an emergency guest. He was back in a second.

"I'll come get you," he said. "Where are you?"

"I'll be sitting on the planter outside my dorm," I said. "They're locking up here."

"Good grief. Okay, I'm on my way."

I trudged out to the planter with my suitcase, hating its cheapness, hating my parents. They had done some dippy, disorganized things in the past, but this was the dippiest. Whoever heard of forgetting that you had a daughter? What on earth would I have done if James's family hadn't been willing to take me in? Gone home with Mrs. Carmichael?

James arrived in a quarter of an hour. I tossed my suitcase in the back of the station wagon. "Isn't this unbelievable?"

He grinned. "Well, they're bound to have their memory jogged when all the other kids in the neighborhood start coming home from college."

"I hope your parents don't mind about this."

"Heck, no. They're looking forward to having you. They love having company anyway and Dad says you're his favorite student."

James's family lived several miles from the college in a brick ranch–style house. The neighborhood

145

had wide streets and big trees. We pulled up through the back yard and parked in the carport next to his father's ancient Mercedes. A small orange tree heavy with fruit stood near a gazebo and a fat cocker spaniel was asleep in the sun. Hearing our car, the spaniel got up, shook itself and came over to us wagging its tail.

James ruffled its fur. "This is Kierkegaard. Kierky for short."

The dog sniffed at me, then went back to his sunny spot and flopped down heavily.

"He's getting pretty old," said James. "He doesn't have a lot of energy these days."

We went in the house through the kitchen. James's mother, her face pink, was pulling cookies out of the oven. Her blond curls were pulled carelessly up on top of her head, some of them tumbling down over her ears. She flashed me a quick smile. "Christmas cookies," she said. "My personal addiction. Want some while they're warm?"

I turned to James abruptly. "How will my parents know where to find me if they do come looking for me?"

Professor Stuart appeared at the kitchen door. He took his pipe out of his mouth. "I've already taken care of that. They'll call the college, I expect, and I've already left word at the college switchboard."

"I hope you like spinach, Dusty," said Mrs. Stuart. "James's dad is planning flounder Florentine for dinner."

"My secret recipe," said Professor Stuart smugly.

"You'll be in the guest room," said James. "Let me show you. Only be sure to tell us if you come

146

up with any fleas because Kierky sometimes sleeps on the bed in there."

A Christmas tree stood next to the grand piano in the family room. It was covered with small ornaments, each of which looked as if it had been in the family for generations. Bookshelves covered the far wall and to the right French doors opened out to the back yard where I could see Kierky sleeping in the sun by the gazebo.

This was the sort of house I would like to have myself—sunny, comfortable, and filled with nicely worn objects that had a history of some kind.

"I love your house," I told James.

All at once I was overcome with a feeling that I was being disloyal to my family even to say that. I tried to think of one thing about my own family's house that I liked as if that would somehow break the spell and I would feel all right again. But I couldn't, of course. I couldn't think of a single thing. In fact, right then it was hard to even think of anything about my family that I liked, much less their house. Maybe that was the problem. Maybe I felt guilty about how angry I was. As much as I had complained about them in my mind, I had never dreamed they would leave me stranded at school. Now it seemed to me that it was crushingly typical of them. It was sort of the quintessence, the ultimate expression of how disorganized they were.

That evening, James's grandmother, a retired opera singer, came for dinner. She was a very grand lady with sallow skin and silver hair put up in an old–fashioned pompadour. She held herself perfectly erect as if she were afraid of breaking. The fingers of her gnarled hands were covered with rings. She seemed very grand.

At dinner, the flounder Florentine was produced with fanfare, Professor Stuart slipping it onto a pre-heated platter. "Go ahead," he urged. "Don't wait for me. Eat it while it's hot."

James shot me an embarrassed glance. I smiled back at him. It was hard for me to understand why James would be embarrassed by his family, but I was familiar enough with the emotion to recognize it when I saw it.

"Dusty," said James's grandmother, fingering the stem of her water goblet. "That's an unusual name for a girl, isn't it?"

"Dusty is my best student," said Professor Stuart, lowering himself into a chair at the head of the table. "I have a twenty-five dollar bet with Professor Shao that she's going to ace the Western Civ. comprehensive next year."

I looked down at my fish and blushed.

After supper, we gathered around the piano and sang Christmas carols. James's grandmother's voice was strong. When she hit the high E on "Hark the Herald Angels Sing," Kierky began to howl.

She glared at him with mock anger. "I have never been able to tolerate critics," she said.

All the next day I kept my ear cocked, half-consciously, listening for my family. Finally, on Sunday morning, they called the Stuarts's house. It had at last occurred to them that I was missing. Dad drove over to St. Pete and picked me up Sunday afternoon.

"My God," he said as we drove off. "What have you done to your hair?"

I touched it gingerly. I had forgotten that it hadn't always been that way. "I bleached it. Do you like it?"

"Why did you do a thing like that? You had such nice hair. Like your mother's."

"I like it better this way."

I was surprised at how comfortable it felt to be sitting in the old car headed for home. The passenger seat in front still leaned at a slant as it had ever since my father's fat Aunt Elsie had sat in it when I was in the ninth grade. The car heater still toasted the driver's right foot while leaving the rest of the interior tepid. But there was a familiar feel and a familiar smell to the old car that felt right. I was past being mad at my family. There was never any point in being mad at them. They were always doing the best they could. They were sort of like some very outdated, narrow gauge railroad train, the kind that showed up in kids' picture books and was called "Tootle." They were never on time, they were completely impractical, but there was a certain goofy charm there. And even courage. No matter how hopeless everything obviously was, they didn't give up. You had to give them that. After a while, I dozed off.

When the car stopped, I saw we were pulling into the driveway of a pink cement block duplex. We could not pull all the way in because Toby's Hot Wheels were blocking the drive.

Dad carried my suitcase inside. "Here's our girl," he announced. "I think she thought we had forgotten about her."

"My God, Deborah Susan," said Mom, her mouth falling open. "What have you done to your hair?"

"The color is called Moonlight Madness. Do you like it?"

"It may take me a while to get used to it." She hugged me. "We certainly blew it this time, didn't we? Frank Jr. said, 'Look at that boy, Mom. I think he's coming back from college. Why isn't Deborah Susan coming back from college?' Ooops! I thought."

"All the commotion with the move and everything, it just completely slipped our mind that you'd be coming home," said Dad. "I don't know what we did with that school calendar you sent us."

Frank Jr. and Toby were in front of the television and did not look up as I took my suitcase past them.

I didn't have to be shown to Peggy's room. It couldn't be the one with the crib next to the bed and it wasn't likely to be the one with the Masters of the Universe figures all over the floor. I unpacked my suitcase in the third bedroom and put my makeup out on top of the bureau. The furniture, at least, was familiar, and the big empty Valentine box that Peggy's boyfriend had given her last year. The overstuffed feeling in the room was familiar, too. It had been a tight squeeze to get Peggy's bed in there. After looking around, I sat down on the bed. That was the only place to sit.

"Well," said Peggy. She stood at the door with her arms folded and looked at my things spread out on the dressing table. "You certainly made yourself at home, didn't you?"

I grinned. "Hey, I'm glad to see you, too."

She sighed. "I'm sorry, but since you've been gone I've had a room to myself for the first time ever and it's been sheer heaven."

"Well, I won't be staying long," I said. "How's school?"

"Just the way you'd think it is when you're jerked away from all your friends in the middle of your junior year and dropped into a snooty, totally alien environment."

"That's tough."

"Well, at least we're not on the bread line," she shrugged. "It could be worse. I like your hair. They warned me not to say anything about it, but I don't think it looks so bad."

Over the sound of the television, I could hear Toby coughing. I remembered then that it was the bronchitis season. It was odd to realize how completely at home I felt. There wasn't even any room at home for me anymore. If anything, this house was smaller than our old one. Peggy was probably counting the minutes until I moved my luggage out. And yet I belonged here. I might change the color my hair, but that was one thing that would never change. I supposed I was a kind of amphibian. Wasn't that what you called someone who could live in two different worlds?

Christmas Day the boys awoke at dawn and tore into their presents in a materialistic frenzy. Peggy and I, as usual, had matching everything. Matching hair dryers. Matching sweaters. Not very much of anything, of course, in view of the family's recent move and Dad's spell of unemployment, but everything we did have was divided perfectly evenly. It was a fetish with my parents. I still remembered the Christmas that I was fifteen when I got a Flintstones bowling set. My parents had obviously sorted out the toys and realized my stack was short, so they lifted the bowling set from Frank Jr.'s stack to even it up.

This Christmas was different, though. I had something that was especially my own—James's present. Opening it very carefully, to prolong the pleasure, I pulled off the top of the tiny white box. In a nest of cotton a gold locket winked at me. I took it out and held it up so that the lights of the Christmas tree were reflected in miniature on the little heart. "Dusty" was inscribed on the front of it in script.

"What's that?" asked Peggy. She leaned over my shoulder to look at it. "Dusty? Who's Dusty?"

I bit my lip trying to subdue a broad smile. "That's me."

JANICE HARRELL is the author of many popular books for both young adult and adult readers. She lives in North Carolina.